STALKED BY THE KRAKEN

LILLIAN LARK

Stalked by the Kraken

Editor: Ellie, My Brother's Editor
Proofreader: Rosa Sharon, My Brother's Editor

To my amazing husband, the Smut Coven,
and the Relief Society.
Tentacles and multiple hearts forever.

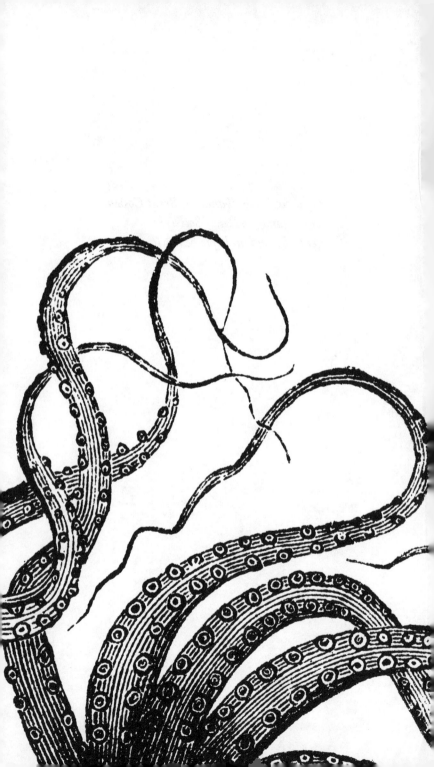

PROLOGUE

GIDEON

The informant slides into the booth across from me, casting a glance around the coffee shop he'd chosen as a meeting location. The light hits the heavy gold jewelry on his fingers and the shine initially pleases my inner creature until he scratches his greasy hair, creating a shower of dandruff. A wave of body spray with a stronger undertone of sweat assaults my senses and immediately puts me off.

Where does Mace find people like this? The man in front of me is *unsavory* in ways I didn't think were a reality anymore.

One of the best things about the modern times, by far, has been the normalization of hygiene. I've lived the majority of my life alongside mortals with varying standards of cleanliness based on the technologies of the time.

But the unsavoriness of the man in front of me is more than the lack of hygiene, which is bad enough, there's an oiliness to his actions. The practiced smile that his poor acting can barely keep on his face. The curl of his lip communicating a discomfort that refuses to be masked.

He has an aura as if he's usually the one coercing people into giving information, not the other way around.

I don't trust him, and now I'm supposed to trust the information he gives me?

"Uh, Moby Dick?"

I want to roll my eyes at the code name Mace has routinely inflicted on me in the past century of our dealings, instead I incline my head in acknowledgment. I should be grateful that this code name hasn't been used for probably a decade. His other favorites are Ahab, Flounder, and when he's feeling especially feisty, Calamari.

If I didn't consider Mace such a good friend, I'd have found a way to sink him to the bottom of the ocean and leave him there. Alas, I'm fond of the bastard.

We haven't done many operations needing secrecy in the past ten years. Our little group mutually decided to slow down on the activities that put targets on our backs and pursue different businesses. But every so often a job comes up where Mace's and my expertise benefit each other.

Perhaps age is slowing us.

The thought would make my lips twitch in a smile if my inner creature wasn't so annoyed by the man's shifty presence. I don't know what this man owes Mace to get him to meet with me but he's obviously unwilling. The air is flavored sour with his distress and anxiety.

I lift my brow in expectation as the informant glances again around the warm, bustling coffee shop. Our identities have been vaguely verified and now comes the time that I get what I'm hunting for. The stalling of this low-level witch does not help with my irritation.

In a different time, a small annoyance would have been enough to perform an act of violence, but the world is no longer in that time and I've changed over the countless years I've wandered.

The informant stills, finally sensing the shift in the air or maybe realizing that I'm more than I appear to be.

"T-That's the place." The informant gestures quickly through the front window of the coffee shop to the storefronts across the street. The stores are an assortment of places from a time gone past. The man could be gesturing to a video rental store with a blinking Open sign. How was that still in business? Or what appeared to be an antique store.

"Which one?" I ask.

The man flinches at my voice but answers, "The antiques place."

"And the goods won't be there until the auction?" I ask.

The informant's nod is shaky and his fingers twitch against the table. All of this stress for a magical artifact auction? Granted, the artifact I'm after was allegedly stolen but the auction itself is technically legal. Unregulated, but legal.

And unless the family contracting with Mace for the retrieval of this artifact goes through the arduous process to prove to the Council officials that it was in fact stolen, the best course of action is to just bid to get the object back.

No paranormal creature wants to involve the Council that governs us all in their business. Especially if the theft was actually some down-on-their-luck family member that sold the artifact under the table; claiming ignorance when the item was noticed to be missing. It's occurred more than once in my line of work.

The job originally came to Mace, who brought me in. I'm the best at tracking down treasure. The artifact in question is an amulet of Byzantine origin that had been passed down through a witch family as an heirloom. Fashioned with silver and some gems, the amulet can act as a magic booster, but the historical nature of it provides most of the value to a collector.

Much to the heir's dismay, the family-line succession requires the possession of the amulet.

I used my contacts to get a list of individuals who authenticate magical items from the Byzantine, and found an expert in this city who claimed to have handled the exact amulet last week. A call to Mace yielded me with a source for the lesser-known businesses in the area. An informant for an auction planned with such an amulet.

"Which is when?" I prod, quickly losing patience with the informant's hand-wringing.

The man names a date that's roughly three weeks from today and I make note of it. The delay is another annoyance, but it's likely if Mace or I contacted the auction hosts, they'd demand triple the worth knowing we were looking to acquire it.

"Can I go now?" he asks. Fear bleeds through his scent. How curious.

I nod, and the man leaves in a rush while still casting looks around. No one was watching us. My creature would have noticed if anyone was paying more than passing attention.

I finish inputting the details for the job into my phone, noting the address for Mace's benefit. He teleported me to this city before taking off, leaving me the keys to one of the many homes the demon keeps. The townhouse is obviously not a place that Mace spends much time in. The air, while being clean, was stale, but the bed is comfortable and the Wi-Fi high speed.

The door to the coffee shop opens again, the sound somehow reaches me over the noise of the espresso machine and clinking of glass. The pull in me is instant. It's as if a strong current sweeps through my chest and my body turns.

A blaze of fire and light catches my eye. My whole being freezes, as stunned as a fish to a lure. The ancient creature in me stirs past the point of wakefulness, past the point of reason, where there is only need and hunger.

Mine.

It takes my thinking brain a moment to interpret the flash as sunlight hitting the hair of a woman entering the coffee shop. She gets to the counter and starts to order in a low voice before I'm recovered enough for my logic to catch up with my nature. My knuckles are white and the table creaks as I attempt to hold myself still.

Never, in all my immortal life, have I felt this demand. Lovers and friends have come and gone with the primal part of myself lazily drifting along to the actions of my two-legged form. We aren't different beings, per se, but rather two halves of a whole.

And the dark part of myself that hides in this civilized world wants *her.*

I watch as the woman's brow creases, and she looks around. Her eyes skip past me. She won't see me until the moment I want her to; my kind are especially skilled at camouflaging our presence.

I take in her appearance. Her hair is a fiery red bordering on orange with curls and flyways that float around her with each movement. Her jewelry catches the light, dangly earrings, small rings on her fingers and thin necklaces delight the part of myself that desires shiny things. Her flowing clothing looks bohemian with small additions of sleekness to modernize it.

I zero in on the woman's face. Her skin is pale with a smattering of freckles visible at a distance. Her lips are pink, and she bites the lower one as the crease in her brow deepens, her eyes narrowing. Can she feel my eyes on her?

More people enter the coffee shop and the woman's face changes from suspicion to surprise. I track her gaze to the two women approaching her with smiles plastered on their faces. Is this an ambush? The energies around me draw in as if to prepare for battle but I relax again when the red-haired woman tilts her head in confusion but warmth.

"What are you guys doing here?" My woman's words travel across the distance easily with my hearing.

My woman?

I shake my head.

Gideon, you can't just claim people as yours on sight. This is a civilized society that requires things like courting and discussion before claims can be made. There's a visceral rejection in me at the inner thoughts. I bow to my instincts even as exasperation flares.

The woman in a green coat answers, "Katherine and I wanted to get coffee with you!"

The other woman, Katherine, nods. "And this is an intervention."

My woman jolts at that. "What?"

Green coat sighs and glares at Katherine. "This is a check-in! Not an intervention."

"Oh." A blush rises on my woman's face.

"Is that okay? We just haven't seen you around the bathhouse lately and wanted to catch up. Lowell said you were over here," green coat says.

I catalog details of the conversation with little context. *Bathhouse? Lowell?*

"Coffee first!" Katherine announces, and the group finishes going through the ordering process at the counter. Talking about the different pastries on offer and making inane comments as if to soothe their target with normalcy but my woman's smile is stiff and her body language whispers of discomfort. Soon the three women take a table not too far away from mine.

I inhale to get a sense of the group. Witches and one… demon. I'll need to be careful around that one, Katherine, could notice my presence if she tried.

"Wanda is right. We've been worried." Katherine's harsh demeanor softens. "How have you been?"

"I've been good," my woman says, her voice cracks with the lie that I taste even at this distance. Wanda and Katherine just stare at her.

"We asked around and none of the regulars have seen much of you for months. Did we do something? Did someone else?" Katherine winces. "Are you avoiding us?"

My woman's eyes widen in horror. "Gods no! Absolutely not."

Katherine and Wanda sigh with relief and guilt wells on my woman's face.

"I just… I haven't really felt like participating lately. I'm taking time to try and get my head on straight. And matching has been crazy—" she cuts herself off. "I haven't really been feeling like myself."

Participating? Matching?

There's a pause.

"Is it about that guy? The one you were seeing." Katherine asks the question carefully but there's venom laced through it. Like she's waiting for one word from my woman to find whoever wronged her and make them pay. I approve.

My woman deflates. "It's stupid."

Wanda snorts. "Feelings are always stupid, but it doesn't make them less valid. If you don't feel like participating in bathhouse fun, then trust that."

My focus narrows. Is this *participating* sexual in nature?

"So, no dating then?" Katherine prods. "No, get-over-one-man-by-getting-under-a-new-one?"

My woman shakes her head in a vicious motion that has her curls bouncing. "Definitely not!"

There's so much horror in her voice, her answer is almost a shriek.

My inner creature writhes at the detail that this woman would not welcome an advance. That is a problem. For some yet unknown reason, it wants her. I want her, and all my intentions of approaching, of courting, halt in my mind.

This will require patience.

Strategy.

"Take your time but don't forget that we all care about you." Wanda shoulder bumps my woman with affection.

I need her name. There's a gnawing ache in my chest to know it.

"And, there are more *options* than men." Katherine waggles her brows. The demoness's action pulls a light snort from my woman. She keeps waggling her brows. "Like retail therapy!"

Now my woman barks a laugh, and a smile pulls at my mouth at the sound.

"That's not where I thought you were going with that," she says.

Wanda frowns, bewildered. "Does shopping usually fix emotional upheaval for you?"

"Well, it doesn't hurt, and it isn't just about buying stuff. It's indulging in items that bring you joy," Katherine says sagely. "Rose, you were practically gushing last we spoke about the limited-edition washi tape the art museum is pushing. Have you already gone to stock up? I saw they just released a few days ago."

"What is washi tape?" Wanda voices my own question, but a detail takes all of my attention.

Rose.

The name matches this woman. Petal soft and color vibrant. If I moved closer and picked up her distinct scent, would it be as lush and floral? My logical self reels in the primal impulse.

"It's decorative tape," Katherine responds.

Rose looks down at the last sips of her drink. "I haven't gotten around to getting any."

The group falls silent for a moment, as if that's an important detail.

"Well, retail therapy it is!" Wanda claps as if fully sold on the positives of shopping now and I admire the care these women are taking with the object of my fascination. The women link arms and playfully drag Rose toward the door.

Right before she steps onto the sidewalk, Rose halts and looks back. My heart rate jumps at the puzzled frown on her face as her eyes move past my position without stopping. Rose shakes her head and allows herself to be pulled along with her friends.

I follow.

The greedy instinct of my creature usually occurs with riches, fine metals, and gems. It works well with my chosen profession. Treasure hunting provides just enough adventure to keep me from getting bored and the glittering results delight my inner self.

I've never hunted a mate before.

CHAPTER 1

One Week Later

ROSE

Someone is watching me.

The air is chilly and pervasive. Fingers of cold reach me despite my brisk pace. I tug the collar of my coat higher around my face. The scratch of the wool against my cheeks is just one more irritating sensation. I fight the urge to look behind me; to make triple sure I'm not being followed.

Don't look. You don't have time for this, Rose.

I suppress the sense of eyes on me that trickles past the cold of the morning and catches my breath. If I do stop, if I do look, I won't see anything more than I have for the past week. Nothing.

No one is following me. No one is watching me.

It's taken days to conclude that my brain is sending faulty signals. As if I need anything else to worry about. Personal turmoil, matchmaking burnout, and now being haunted by eyes that aren't there.

My destination comes into view and my worries ease. A nondescript storefront bordered by other nondescript stores. This year our place of business masquerades as a video rental location.

I'd argued against it. Argued that the novelty of the business would be more noticeable than if it was just another antique store that no one visits. But the storefront next to us had been bought out by an actual antique store, so my vote was vetoed.

Our building is so heavily spelled that the only individuals who enter The Love Bathhouse are those who mean to enter. Through all the generations that my family have run the bathhouse, we've never had an unsuspecting human stumble through our door. And to suggest otherwise would insult the ward master we contract with, so I keep my misplaced worries to myself.

I open the glamoured door and step into the lobby. The sizzle of magic and warmth is a homecoming over my skin. My steps echo off the marble floors to the arched mosaic ceiling.

Lowell smiles lazily at me from the front desk. My cousin's rust-colored hair sticks every which way but it's the manner he sprawls back in his chair that has my lips tugging up. Well, at least one of us is relaxed.

"You look like you've had a good morning." My words are wry.

A family business built around sex magic is a practice in avoidance, and in knowing too many intimate details anyway. Thank the gods Jared never participates. I don't want to know anything of that nature about my brother.

The worst I've had was being walked in on by my mother—scratch that—the time I walked in on my parents was worse. We all gave a collective cheer when they retired early and moved to the coast.

Lowell is in a different category than immediate family. He's one of my closest friends. His details about conquests don't make me feel squeamish. Most times anyway. Lowell is an open person who can forget we're related when he gets too excited.

My cousin's smile goes dreamy at the edges. "Katherine came in right when I opened. She had a bad night and needed someone to take the edge off."

I snort. Katherine is the best sort of regular to have. Succubi need sex to live. Our business needs sex to turn a profit. The bathhouse manager participating though… it's not against the rules, but it isn't in his job description.

I lean in to pry. "So, you and Katherine?"

The tops of Lowell's ears redden, and I bite back a smile. The urge to smile dies a slow death as Lowell avoids my gaze and furrows his brow.

Oh.

I wait and give my cousin the space to ask whatever question he's trying to make himself ask. What I'm dreading he'll ask.

Finally, Lowell unclenches his jaw. "I was wondering if you could tell me… how good of a match are we? Do you think…" He takes a deep breath. "Is there a chance?"

My throat tightens and I try to keep my breathing measured, to beat back the recent anxiety plaguing me. I stall and take in the glossy tile work of the lobby instead of my cousin's hopeful face.

Just a few months ago I would have answered Lowell with utmost confidence. Pondering matches is what I do.

Did.

Do. Fuck it, I'm the best matchmaker the witching world has seen in decades. I have the skills and capabilities that uniquely make my matches so successful. One bad match shouldn't destroy my confidence in the whole process.

I still make matches. Just last week I made a match that I'd give the metric of being eighty percent perfect and I received an email last night from the gargoyle-witch pair wanting to schedule their first session in the bathhouse. A successful match indeed.

My measuring system can't be broken down into exactitudes, but I rate with numbers because I tell myself that numbers don't lie. I used to pride myself in having an unbiased matching system before—I shake my head at the thoughts about the issues in my process and bring myself to the matter of the vivacious Katherine, my friend who ambushes me just to check in, and my favorite cousin.

I don't need to read Lowell's soul threads. I see soul threads constantly and have an uncanny memory for their patterns, their movements. Everyone has a different pattern. The very being of their soul reaches in one direction or another, dancing in the ether. Some even just plain reach for what they desire; those are the easy matches.

Lowell's soul threads are a glowing orange in my mind's eye. They lazily sway like a slow burning fire or golden wheat in a field. Katherine's threads, in contrast, are a swirling scarlet, spinning in a hungry dance. The beat of their soul song, the rhythm of their threads, only seldom occurs in harmony; only to scatter away from the other's timing.

"Ten percent maybe." The words are like ash in my mouth. I avoid looking at Lowell, but I don't need to look to feel the disappointment echoing from him.

My shoulders drop. "I'm sorry, Lowell. You could still give it a go. You know my methods aren't foolproof."

"Not foolproof, but accurate most of the time."

The words come out a little sad but sure and I envy that. Confidence. As my own certainty dwindles, the more other's confidence in anything chafes.

The doubt started small months ago and has only compounded, growing until it suffocates me. Avoidance is all I can do to breathe sometimes.

"I didn't even know you were interested in being matched," I say, trying to keep from more uncomfortable introspection about my issues.

Or the fact that I do have a compatible match in mind for Lowell, one that's solid to ground Lowell's laid back airy nature, but the suggestion sticks in my mouth. The person in question hasn't shown an interest in being matched and the possibility of the match going poorly has me taking the coward's way out.

Silence.

"I guess I am. I was going to ask you before..." Lowell tapers off.

"The Jackson incident?" I twist my mouth. Uncomfortable introspection seems to be the name of the game today.

"Yeah, that. I held off after everything went down."

My shoulders drop even lower and an ache fills my chest. How is it surprising that I've lost the trust of others? It's hard even trusting my own methods now. Would the word get out soon? How long until people stop coming to me to match them altogether?

"Hey." Lowell's voice is sharp. "Stop thinking whatever is going through your head right now."

I start at his tone and he nods.

"I held off because you haven't seemed like yourself. I didn't want to add more to your plate when I'm not a hundred percent sure I want to be in a relationship," Lowell says. "It's just that the thought of having someone is… nice."

Having someone does sound lovely.

"Not because I'm a fuckup?" I ask.

Lowell snorts at that. "Perfectionist much? One time, you're wrong one time, for the best let me tell you, and you've labeled yourself a fuckup. Be a little kinder to yourself."

Frustration spikes in me. "It's not just that I messed up. It's that my method proved itself entirely flawed—"

"In one incredibly rare case." Lowell glares at me. "That doesn't mean your methods are useless now."

I bite my lip. I've spent so much time mulling over the Jackson incident in my head that I don't know what to believe.

"That asshole was an outlier," Lowell says. I can recognize that he's using my preferred vocabulary to soothe me, but it still works.

An outlier.

"You're still the best in the business so I'll trust your prediction about Katherine. I mean." Lowell's devil-may-care grin eases some of my tight frustration. "For a committed relationship anyway."

The sound of the front door opening has both of us straightening and I'm not even on desk duty.

The woman who enters walks in as if she owns the place and my mouth quirks. My attention is captured by her unique soul pattern. Gold threads stretch into the world, tangling around everything in sight. A shadow of golden wings lifts from her back, invisible to the insensitive individual.

Wings? Not a seraph or any other celestial creature I've met. The energy and wings they have are different. This woman's energy feels more *feral*. I straighten when the answer occurs to me, it rings through me with the same instinct that other witches describe as *the knowing*. Surprise blooms at the confirmation, I'm not a witch that is graced with *the knowing* often.

I've never met a harpy before.

The harpy takes in the lobby, turning in a slow circle and tilting her head back to look at the decorative arches. Her lips part slightly at the winding geometric designs and a prideful warmth fills me. Our bathhouse is a gorgeous space.

The flavor of the décor is a surprise for newcomers. The style is a mix between lush pinks and striking whites; not quite Turkish bathhouse, and not quite modern facility, but some warm combination.

The harpy's focus snaps back to Lowell and me, as if forcing herself away from the décor. Lowell jolts when the woman's gaze hits him, and I wonder if Katherine is so soon forgotten or if this woman is just stunning enough to distract my cousin for the moment.

"How can we help you?" Lowell asks.

The woman makes it to the front desk. Her green eyes shine with mischief and suspicion creeps up my spine. Most newcomers are just curious about our business, a fraction stay and become regulars, and a small number bring ugly things in. Judging our business as shameful. Which kind of newcomer will this harpy be?

"A friend of mine gave me this location, but they were… brief when describing the services you offer." Her fingers slide over the intricately carved front desk. The carving is one I have practically memorized from my younger days

manning the front desk and leaves no mystery of the type
of business an individual has entered.

The pretty floral pattern includes numerous figures
copulating in many different, some quite creative,
positions. My great-grandmother designed it.

The harpy's eyebrows lift and her hands flit to the
business cards instead, picking up mine.

"Rose Love, Matchmaker. Is that really your last name?
Love?" she asks, her mouth twists in amusement.

I smile back in good humor, the joke isn't funny after
living it my whole life but it's better to just share in the
mirth.

"The Love Bathhouse has been in my family for
generations. We don't quite know if the bathhouse or the
last name came first, it's a detail lost to time." I stick my
hand out for a professional handshake. "I'm Rose, and you
are?"

The harpy takes my hand.

"Sophia Shirazi—" she cuts off in abrupt surprise.

My smile goes sly. "Ah, we should have warned you.
The building has many spells working in it, and we don't
allow for aliases here. Informed consent between partners
or among parties is something we take very seriously."

Sophia's scowl is light at best. Her excitement is too
tangible to compete with the inconvenience of giving her
real name and most of my suspicion falls away.

"So, this bathhouse is for…" She trails off.

"Hosting consensual sexual acts between two or more
adults." Lowell answers quickly before I can. "Lowell
Carter, I'm the bathhouse manager."

"Oh, you don't get the Love name?" Sophia teases.

"Sadly, I'm a mere distant relation," Lowell says gravely.

I roll my eyes. Lowell could change his name if he wanted to. My mother had tried to convince him to change it on many occasions, but he hadn't wanted to be boxed into working in the family business before now.

"If I wanted to partake in such services how much would it cost?" Sophia bats her eyelashes at Lowell. My cousin blushes and I can't help smiling at his expense.

"Oh, we don't provide those kinds of services," I cut in. "You couldn't, say, demand that Lowell service you for a fee."

Lowell clears his throat, glaring at me as his blush darkens. "Quite."

I continue, easing up on my teasing so I don't get hit with one of Lowell's pranks in retribution later. "Rather, our system is that we provide the space, either a private or a public room for sexual acts to occur. We don't take money for providing the space and we don't provide individuals for any sexual acts."

Sophia blinks in confusion.

"The spaces are set to absorb the raw magic produced from sexual acts," I say. "The other side of our business is to sell that magic to help power spells or defenses that witches and others need to perform their own businesses. We work in partnership with some of the largest warding companies that exist."

"Clever," Sophia breathes out. "So you provide the space for affairs?"

I make a sound of disagreement. Is this why she's here?

"Our spaces can be used for that purpose. It isn't our favored function, but we try to provide judgment-free spaces." I shrug. "Since we do keep records and don't allow aliases, the more popular option, what our regulars come back for, is our group and public space options for those with certain tastes."

"Kinky," Sophia says, her brows lifting.

Lowell jumps in with his usual pitch, his cheeks merely pink now. "Kinky public groups are currently on Tuesdays and Wednesdays. Sodomy Saturday has become very popular, but it's suggested you BYOP, bring your own partner, for that. We also suggest spelling leathers against moisture as the bathhouse is a functional bathhouse and quite humid even in the public baths."

Sophia turns back to me. "And you matchmake for these events?"

"Yes and no. I can match just sexual partners, but my main clientele are those looking for long-term partners." I pause. "Or groups. Are you looking to be matched?"

Sophia's energies are all over the place and powerful. Matching her would be a challenge. I wouldn't even be able to rely on species compatibility since I have a sense that Sophia's wildness wouldn't want to be confined to another harpy.

Sophia's eyes widen in comical panic. "Oh, no! Not me! I'm not interested in… being matched."

There seems to be more nuance to her answer, but it's eluding me. I shrug. I have plenty of individuals looking for love. I don't need to go out of my way to match someone that doesn't want it.

"Well then!" Lowell opens a drawer in the front desk and pulls out some papers. "Here are some pamphlets that may answer some questions you haven't thought to ask yet."

"But—" Sophia interrupts and winces. "Uh, say I have a friend who would be interested in being matched. How does that work?"

I'm having the hardest time getting a read on this woman but I answer.

"Your friend would have to come in or send a video of them introducing themselves to the email I list on that business card. Then I'll onboard them with the expectations." As I explain, the burden of my full inbox weighs on me. So many people wanting to be matched. My indecision is causing a pile up.

I clear my throat. "Generally we ask for a commitment, if they are successfully matched, to three intimate sessions in the bathhouse. Our preference is for the first time the match is intimate, as it is the most potent time, but we're flexible and understand that every match is different."

"They'd have to have sex in public?" Sophia squeaks out her question.

Lowell turns his face to hide his smile, but I politely respond.

"If that is the preference of the matched, but most use our private rooms."

"Oh, uh, thank you." She nods to me and picks up the papers Lowell slid toward her. "Would I be able to get a tour?"

Lowell good-naturedly waggles his eyebrows. "Only if you're willing to sign the forms and read all the rules right now."

Sophia hesitates with a hum. "Maybe next time then."

I don't follow the rest of the conversation because a man walks into the lobby. His energy harried and worried.

"Jared?" I step out from behind the front desk and toward my brother.

"We need to talk," he says.

CHAPTER 2

GIDEON

I tap my fingers one by one against the countertop. The motion is measured. Controlled. Only the inexperienced hunter lets themselves fidget. No matter that impatience is stringing me tight.

The empty coffee mug clinks in the saucer with each impact. I stop and look through the window at the video rental store my mate had entered earlier and catch sight of the harpy crossing the street toward the coffee shop. Relief unwinds and I breathe a little deeper. Soon. I'll know more soon.

I've circled Rose for the past week, not daring to enter her heavily spelled place of business disguised as the rental store without knowing more. Her business and home are the only places she goes that I don't watch her. I do have some boundaries, no matter how much the primal part of me wants to see her in those spaces. It wants confirmation that the men who enter her home are, in fact, members of her family as I suspect.

Perhaps I should have approached her already, enacted a plan or investigated her life. But investigating isn't how I want to learn all the details about Rose and something about simply watching Rose eat a croissant on a park bench or slowly browsing at the library is soothing. That she exists is enough for me. It's not enough for my creature though.

That part of me is impatient to have a plan.

My phone lights up on the counter with a call. The contact information disappears when I reject it. I'll contact the nosy demon later. Right now, I have more important things that require my attention.

Things like the tricky Sophia Shirazi taking the stool next to mine at the counter.

"You were quick," I say, keeping my gaze on the storefront.

"You only wanted the most basic information. Don't insult me."

I stop my mouth from quirking. We only just met, and I already know that I like this harpy. I had been given her contact info a few weeks ago and kept it on hand in case I needed something and didn't want to use my usual channels.

As it happened, I had use of her services much earlier than I anticipated. Mostly because I didn't want to hear what Mace thought of my request.

"And?"

"Such an interesting business model they have over there." Sophia slides a couple of pamphlets over. Informational-type papers detailing business hours and FAQs. The harpy proceeds to explain the details of The Love Bathhouse.

Each detail illuminates the conversation I overheard among Rose and her friends a little more.

It's a rather neat operation they're running. It's not unique, sex bathhouses have been a thing for thousands of years, I've visited a few in my younger days. But the selling of raw magic to finance it is a rather delightful modernization of the concept. It also gives me an in.

"And Rose?" I ask.

"Rose Love is a matchmaker." Sophia slides over a business card with dark gold lettering. I pick the card up and I let the light catch the metallic ink.

"A matchmaker?" As old of a profession as sex bathhouses and one that comes with respect and standing in a community. There is a lack of order and unity in the paranormal world and many communities of creatures are flung wide. In times gone past, having an official facilitate matches was an invaluable way to avoid conflict and unnecessary acts of conquest. I have no doubt the position is still a valued one, even during the precarious peace the paranormal world has accomplished.

"She matches people, and in exchange those people use the bathhouse for their first 'intimate' moments."

I tilt my head. Very interesting.

"Is that all you were able to get?" I dig.

Sophia's face scowls before smoothing. "A dark-haired man named Jared showed up after I spoke to her. They went back to what I'm assuming is her office in a hurry."

Violence swells in my chest, but I suppress the bloody instinct. It takes a moment. It's a moment that Sophia watches carefully, but finally I relax my body. If there is competition for my Rose, I will deal with it.

It only means that I need to make my entrance sooner rather than later. Patience may be key for a hunter, but so is knowing when to strike.

"Anything else?" I ask.

"Anything else you want to know?"

I pick up my phone and make the money transfer.

"No, but a little advice. In the future, get your clients to pay upfront."

A blush steals up Sophia's neck, but she glares at me. "Will do."

With a haughty flip of her hair, the harpy departs.

I'm pleased. In time I can see Sophia doing very well in this business. If her family allows it, harpies are known to be a protective bunch.

My phone lights up with a text.

Mace: Answer my call or I'm going to show up there

I curse, with his abilities, the threat isn't an idle one. I answer the call. "Yes?"

"You ignore my call and now you're acting like I'm the one inconveniencing you."

"You are inconveniencing me," I grind out. This conversation is currently the only thing keeping me from finally going after Rose.

"Now that's just rude. I get one email last week and—"

"What do you want, Mace?"

"I can't just want to hear my friend's voice?"

"I'm hanging up."

"No! Wait! Your email lists a date for the auction that isn't for another two weeks. Are you sure?"

I snort. "As sure as the informant you set up is."

Mace huffs. "And that's what I don't like."

I shake my head, not surprised by the statement. Mace actually knows details about the man we're supposed to be trusting.

Mace continues, "What if they move the date up? We'll completely miss it and won't have a clue. It's not like we're actually invited guests."

I debate my response for a second. "I'm going to be in the area. I'll keep an eye out."

There is a pause on the other side of the phone, and I roll my eyes.

"Will you now? May I ask why?"

I purse my lips. "Something has caught my interest."

My inner self rebels at the thought of a competing male coming anywhere near my mate until I ensnare her for myself. The impulse is ridiculous, but there anyway.

"Something in that rainy city has caught your interest? Enough that you'll be there for a full two weeks? I'm curious…"

Nosy demon is nosy, how unsurprising.

I sigh. "I'll let you know. Later."

Right now I have a mate to catch.

CHAPTER 3
ROSE

"That can't be right." My ears ring with disbelief, but Jared's voice still reaches me, echoing through my office.

"I've run all the numbers, multiple times. We've been lower than expected on raw magic the last couple of months. This month is the worst. If we don't change something, we won't be able to fill our current commitments."

Jared hesitates. My brother, the businessman, never hesitates.

"The only differences I can find is a small decrease in the number of regulars attending the baths, which is normal for this time of year, and... a major decrease in the matches you make."

That knocks the breath out of me, and I shake my head.

"No. I've made fewer matches, but I made sure to make the minimum number required to bring in new individuals to replace the outflow." As much as we'd love it, regulars don't stay regular forever. It's a community but there's always an organic ebb and flow to it.

Jared runs a hand through his hair in frustration. "Rose, I know you increased the metric of compatibility for those being matched. I even get why, I do, but I'm telling you that we've had plenty of successful matches in the past where you only predicted a fifty percent compatibility and have had a major downturn in collected magic."

My throat swells.

Jared takes in my silence before continuing, "I'm running an investigation. Top to bottom of the business. There might be something else going on, some compounding factor, because you've always made more matches than prior matchmakers." Jared shrugs. "But we've also been more aggressive with the number of orders accepted to move the amount of raw magic we've had on hand."

Magic doesn't store especially well so it's always been better to sell it quickly for the best efficiency.

"If this is a flaw in how many orders we're accepting, I will deal with it." Jared's voice is full of confidence, but he gentles it. "In the meantime, if you could make more matches until the investigation reaches a conclusion, I'd really appreciate it."

I nod, but numbness makes the gesture stilted. "I'll take another look through possible matches. I just… I was trying to be careful."

Jared takes my hand and squeezes it. My brother is astute, and he isn't heartless. He can guess the reasons behind my actions and in some distant way I'm aware that he'll support the decisions I make about matches. But the business… the business is a cold mistress.

I'd rather resign than let my failure of confidence dent our family business. There are other matchmakers in the world, but not many to choose from.

I fortify myself with a breath.

"I'll make more matches," I say. Trying to imbue conviction in my tone.

My brother's harsh features soften. "Thank you, Rose. I need to get back to the office and start the overhaul. I'm bringing in an independent investigator to compare their results with my own. We'll get to the bottom of this. I just need some time."

I stand when he does and catch him in a hug. He squeezes me back.

"I know it was hard for you to tell me this," I say into his coat. "But I really appreciate you doing it. For trusting that I can handle it."

We break our hug at the same time.

"Always, Rose. This is our business. I'll be talking to Lowell too before I go, just in case there is some evaluation he can make of the bathhouse process."

Jared leaves and I try to let the warm colors and lush décor of my office ground me. This is my sanctuary. I rarely meet with clients in person, so this space is my own. I picked out everything from the lovely, incredibly suggestive art on the walls to the plush rug under my feet. My desk is another of my great-grandmother's designs, a carved monstrosity inspired by Dante's circles, fiery images of copulating figures instead of the pretty floral design in the lobby.

The desk was originally in my father's office around the corner from the bathhouse, but Jared had absolutely refused to keep the desk in the office he inherited. I love it. It dwarfs the space but it's sturdy and always makes me smile. The glossy surface is clear of everything but my laptop, a select number of candles, and some carefully placed items from my stationery collection. The intention is that the pretty marble paper with gold art deco designs is at the ready for me to dive into my work.

All I have to do is reach out for it.

I use pen and paper to help direct my magic. It's a method of meditation that connects with me. Something about the sensation of the drag of the ink across paper is aligning. It's my go-to process for more difficult matches, past the point of reading soul threads.

The connection to all things paper products has bloomed into a passion and my collection of stationery, pens, and the like is meticulously organized and displayed along one wall of my office. My multi-color hoard of treasures.

I should make a list. Use the pretty paper on my desk instead of hesitating. Pull out the new washi tape from the shopping trip with Katherine and Wanda. The tape that I put in a drawer, that I haven't been able to make myself touch.

The top item that I'll write on my list will be *Be brave, make more matches.*

I clench my hands into fists and try to commit to the action. Commit to sitting down to work. Commit to matching hopefuls together. Individuals who want to find someone to hold in the night and plan futures with; have families with.

Like what I wanted before—

A knock on the doorframe startles me. The interruption to the downward spiral of my thoughts is welcome.

I freeze at the sight of the man in the doorway. The air around him crackles and my body tenses in a way that makes it hard to breathe.

"I told the man who just left that I was looking for the matchmaker and he said I should just come straight in.

Is that alright?" His deep voice rolls over me. It's gentle and low, as if to keep a pond of water from rippling. It has a softness that could be an accent, though not a recognizable one.

The concept of tall, dark, and handsome is such a friendly stereotype compared to the reality of the man in front of me. Tall, yes, and he does have dark hair, dark eyes too, but handsome… is such a weak word.

His face, his form, isn't appealing; it's arresting.

His presence is the definition of a distraction.

A small smile curves his mouth and I'm startled out of my reverie, blinking.

Of course my enterprising brother would send the man to me. The power levels coming off this stranger by his mere presence has a static itch running over my scalp. The power yielded if I can match him… we wouldn't need to worry about not being able to fill orders.

"Yes, of course. I'm Rose Love, the matchmaker. Let me take your coat."

I don't usually take people's coats for them. This isn't a formal establishment. People can hang their own items on a coatrack. I don't know why I do it, but I can't regret the offer.

I step close to the stranger and breathe in his scent. He smells like the rain from outside, green things, and salt. My fingers coast over the top of his shoulder before gripping his coat. The man slides out of the garment with ease, as if he's done such a formal gesture hundreds of times.

The stranger is dressed in a simple dress shirt and pants. My palms itch to run over the smooth-looking fabric of his shirt, to feel the warmth of his skin.

Stop lusting after a man wanting to be matched, Rose!

This is business. I've been attracted to clients I've matched before, but never act on it. *Participating* with bathhouse patrons is acceptable, but matching clients are looking for relationships and I try to stay impartial for them.

I need to focus. I shut the door of my office because it helps with my… focus.

"Please, take a seat." I gesture to a plush chair before sitting down behind my desk.

My mouth goes dry as I take him in, and I swallow. His dark eyebrows lift, and I want to shake off this ridiculous interest kindling in my blood. This man is not for me. Matching doesn't work for me.

A perfect match is rare. And once a perfect match is found, there isn't much use in looking anymore. And when that perfect match rejects the partner?

How can anyone trust the matchmaking method after that?

I push onward, refusing to listen to doubts, refusing to think about my personal failure.

"How can I help you, Mr.…."

I frown as something that has been tickling in the back of my brain finally registers. The man in front of me doesn't have soul threads, none that are visible to me anyway. There is no technicolor, dancing display for me to read.

No way for me to match this man to anyone.

CHAPTER 4

ROSE

"Strand, Gideon Strand."

His voice thrums along my nerves and I fight to keep from leaning in. There's a pause in the conversation and I jump to fill it.

To do my job.

"Well, Mr. Strand—"

"Gideon, please." He tilts his head before shaking it. "I'm interested in participating in the endeavor of this establishment."

Gideon's words have me pausing. I struggle to follow what he's saying, he's phrasing it in such a strange way. We usually call performing sexual acts that contribute to the harvesting of magic *participating*, but he's in my office. He's come to a matchmaker, so he must want to be matched.

I try again to see the threads around Gideon, squinting for good measure, aiming to see his soul winding out for others but it's no use. It's as if a void exists where he is and all I'm left with is the staticky feel of his power filling the room.

Frustration creases my forehead. However much we need raw power, I have to refuse to match him. It wouldn't be right to get his hopes up.

"Well, Gideon." I take an inappropriate amount of pleasure in saying his name. "While I'd be pleased to have you *participate* in this establishment, I'm afraid I won't be able to find you a match, if that is what you're wanting."

"No need to find me a match, I already have a woman in mind for this arrangement."

"Oh, you do?" The sharp ache of jealousy takes me by surprise. *Stop it. You barely know him. This man is not for you.*

But then… why is he meeting with a matchmaker?

A glint shines in Gideon's eyes, as if he can read my thoughts.

"I understand that the usual arrangement for your business is to provide a place for sexual encounters in exchange for siphoning off magic to be sold. I'm sure you can tell that the amount of magic I have to offer from such an interaction would be substantial."

I clear my throat. "Yes. But if you already have a partner you don't need to meet with me. I merely arrange the best matches I can."

"I disagree, I do need to meet with you"—Gideon's voice deepens— "because you're the one I want to be my partner."

His eyes seem to darken and the intense look of heat that flashes in them has my body tightening.

It takes me a full second to comprehend his words.

My mouth drops open.

"What?" I squeak.

Gideon leans back, his legs crossed and fingers clasped. Confidence personified. I try hard to tame my tongue into making words, corral my brain into some semblance of order.

"I'd like to enter into an agreement where we are matched," he says.

The way my body heats is a purely physical response.

"You'd want me to be matched with you? But…" My words trail off and I'm trying to grab hold of my thoughts before they scatter. Scatter at the mere hint of thinking about what an arrangement with Gideon would include.

"You'd agree that an interlude between us would be excellent for your business."

My cheeks begin to burn, and a bad taste fills my mouth.

"I don't have sex with clients in exchange for magic."

And I don't. When I decide to have sex in the bathhouse, it's purely for enjoyment, not as an *exchange*. No matter what others might assume about me.

Pain mixes with embarrassment.

Gideon's eyes widen for a moment before speaking. "I've offended you. I'm going about this wrong."

"Are you?" My voice sounds thin. A fragile thing with sharp brittle edges.

Gideon's dark eyes are direct. "My nature is greedy."

Many paranormal beings speak of the otherness as their *nature*. Despite everything, my curiosity piques. What is this man? He must be ancient from the power coming off of him.

"It wants what it wants, and that's you."

That tone, I refuse to interpret his words in any way that makes me believe I'm special even if his focused words hint at that.

"Why me?"

Gideon opens his mouth but snaps it shut. He clears his throat and looks away, as if the question is a hard one, before answering.

"Why not you?" Gideon shrugs, his tone cavalier, like it doesn't matter. Like I'm an afterthought.

See, Rose, not special. Convenient. I snort, but the humor isn't there. "How romantic."

Every word this man says cuts and I've already felt like a walking wound that refuses to heal for months. I don't need this kind of pain.

I stand and walk to my office door and open it. "I think we're done."

Gideon moves slowly. Not slow in a lumbering, clumsy way, but in a deliberate way that quickens my breath.

"I listen to my instincts, Rose. They have never led me wrong."

I scoff at that. What a luxury for him to never have the experience of being led astray by *instincts*. Not like I have. My emotions are a clash of contrasting colors that gray into bitterness.

"Well, that's great for you."

Gideon takes his coat off the rack and steps in front of me. The heat of his body has mine responding. My foolish body hasn't gotten the message that we are not on board with going down this road. Warmth curls in my belly.

"The magic isn't meant to be a payment, just a benefit. There are a host of other benefits to us coming together." Gideon's words are seductive, and I have to steel myself from gravitating toward them.

My exhale is shaky, and the corners of Gideon's lips tick up before he winces.

"There are also some things you might consider undesirable. Things I'd want to talk with you about. Things that may require the *enticement* of benefits. I'm not in the habit of using sweet words, little witch. I apologize if I've upset you—"

I scoff at that, but my mind is already spinning. *Undesirable?*

Gideon continues. "—It was not my intention. I'll admit I can have a one-track mind in matters of desire. If you were amenable to an agreement between us, I swear that you would be the one to navigate our course. Please, call me should you reconsider."

A white card appears between us and I take it without thinking. Or rather, while thinking of all the benefits of the two of us coming together. Sweaty, gasping benefits.

Gideon doesn't immediately release the card. His face moves near mine and he inhales as if scenting me. The action is a quick one, and then I'm the only one holding the paper. It should have been creepy, but a flush wraps around me, a tightening bind clutching my body before releasing.

Gideon leaves and my heart pounds in time to his quick step.

Rose said no.

A normal man may be disappointed, but the rejection invigorates me.

Because now I've officially met my mate. Now, I know that Rose wants me.

Her desire showed in the way her eyes dilated, the quickening of her heartbeat, and the way her lips parted just so. I hoarded every detail. Greedily consumed being near my mate for the first time.

Being close to Rose was a distraction I hadn't counted on. Along with the small signs of Rose's desire, there were the details that my hunter senses hadn't picked up on during my slow stalking. The small golden freckles that dotted near her lashes, the way the hazel of her eyes darkened with the turbulent emotions I inspired.

Even her scent is a bright thing, calling to my creature. Like walking through a lemon grove full of sunlight.

The distraction made me clumsy. The experience is a novel one.

I could blame my blunder on rushing in when Sophia told me about the man who met with Rose, but I won't make excuses. I suspect that the dark-haired man who directed me to her office is a relation. They have the same color of eyes and I've seen him and the man at the front desk with the same shade of hair as Rose's visiting her home.

I can't afford to be so clumsy next time. And there will be a next time. I'll give Rose some time to reconsider before making my next move. I sensed the curiosity there. I stirred it strategically to draw out my mate.

Small movements, tiny influences, until I can surround my Rose and claim her.

I politely wave a farewell to the man at the front desk on my way out. He gives me a lazy perusal and a wave.

I exit the front doors and start down the sidewalk before the sight of a familiar figure leaning against a lamppost creates a hitch in my step. I mentally curse and keep walking.

"What an interesting business for you to visit." Mace sounds smug and my mood worsens. Mace continues, "I mean, it does make sense to scope it out since it's right next to the target location but there seems to be more going on."

I growl.

"You sounded so annoyed with me on the phone that I just figured I should check in on you."

I scoff. "You're here to check in on me? Not because you're a nosy bastard?"

Mace's smile spills with delight. "Well, that too. It's not like it's a bother to stop by and see an old friend."

Damn demon with the damned ability to teleport. The ability is so rare for any creature that I never thought of it as a detraction to aligning with Mace until now.

"Don't you have better things to do? What about bothering Asa? It feels like ages since I've had to pull the two of you out of a clusterfuck."

Mace sighs. "Asa is enjoying mated bliss. He's turned boring."

That stops my steps. "Asa's mated? When did that happen?"

Mace's mood improves at the chance to gossip. "He met a nice wolf-shifter a month ago. They aren't using official titles like 'mate' yet, but Asa is sure of him."

I make a sound of thought. "Good for him."

Mace blinks at me. "Ah."

"What?"

"You've met someone."

I press my lips in a tight line, turning away to continue walking without a destination.

"Whenever I've brought up matters of people mating before, you've been utterly dismissive. Big, grumpy monster you are. 'Mace.'" He drops his voice into a low, gruff range in a terrible impression of me. "'Why would I care who is sleeping with who?' And now you're just like 'Good for him.' That's just fishy."

I roll my eyes, but stay silent.

"Sooo? Who is she? When can I meet her? You know I'll find a way to meet her, so it's better to just introduce us."

There is a small constriction in my throat. "She isn't quite aware of my intentions yet."

Mace stops walking and I leave him behind, trying to escape from his scrutiny.

He catches up too soon.

"Gideon, you've been in this area close to a week now. Don't lie to me and say it's just been for tourism." After a moment where I don't respond, Mace groans. "Have you been following her? We live in a modern age, Gid. You can't just stake out a woman and hunt her down like a target."

"Can I point out that whatever you may think about ancient times, that was not the method then any more than it is now. Virgin sacrifices made hunting women unnecessary," I quip.

Mace pauses, trying to decipher whether I'm making a joke or not. I am, but he doesn't need to know that. Some hesitancy would be good for him.

Mace shakes his head and gets back on topic. Pity. "You haven't responded to my question."

Because I don't want to. But the demon is just going to keep badgering me. Or find Rose himself. And the mere thought of that makes my mind roil with a violence that I'd regret acting on.

"I'm being… careful." As careful as I'm picking my words right now. "My creature is obsessed with her. It's never been like this before. My need is… I don't want to ruin things. So, I'm being cautious in my courting."

"You're hunting." Mace's voice is flat. "Making no sudden movements until you plan to strike."

I clear my throat but don't respond.

Mace makes a disgusted sound. "Just try to remember that she's a woman and not a skittish fish. I want this to work out for you."

Me too.

CHAPTER 5

ROSE

I don't throw away the business card. My fingers itch to, but every time I pick it up off my desk to toss into the garbage, my calluses catch on the textured paper and his name stops me. *Gideon Strand.*

The man can't have been as attractive as I remember, but something tells me he's even more.

A few hours later and the business card is looking less and less like an unsavory proposition and more like a lifeline. A way to stall myself from making a bad match.

It's silly. I've been matchmaking officially since my twenty-first birthday. My skills made themselves known in high school, but no one wants a teenager matching them except other teenagers.

I've successfully matched countless couples. Some at even less than a fifty percent compatibility.

And now, now I can't even comprehend making such big decisions about people's lives unless I'm certain. The what-ifs plague me. What if it doesn't work out for them? What if they destroy each other? What if one gets more hurt than the other?

I had a hundred percent compatibility match and that was a disaster.

Frustration has me leaving my office. I can't look at names and videos any longer. It isn't helping. All the easy matches have already been made.

Lowell smiles at me from the front desk and I scowl back.

His smile widens. "Oh, hello, little storm cloud."

The name throws me off for a second. Gideon called me *little witch* as he was leaving, I liked the endearment too much.

"Why are you still on desk duty?" My bad mood should be contagious, but Lowell is immune.

"Sandra went into labor before her shift this morning."

"Oh! That's wonderful!" It's a breath of fresh air to think about someone else instead of my own issues. My issues are still in the back of my mind because I matched Sandra to her mate. They gave a speech thanking me at the baby shower we had for her. The speech had been beautiful and distressing all at the same time. What if I'm slowly losing my ability to match people altogether?

"Wait, didn't you hire someone for her maternity leave?" I ask.

"They don't start until next week. I don't mind manning the front desk. It lets me think."

My smile is small. "Oh no, anything but that."

The frustration that drove me out of my office slowly drains away and I take a seat next to Lowell.

"Do you want to talk about it?" he asks. He knows me so well.

"That I'm broken and can't match people anymore?"

My cousin's eyebrows lift. "Well, I was asking about tall, dark, and broody but if you want to talk about your lost mojo, we can start with that."

I hum. Of course Lowell had checked him out.

"Gideon Strand," I say.

"That's a nice name."

"He wants to make an agreement for bathhouse sessions."

"Oh really?" Lowell wags his eyebrows in suggestion.

"With me."

There's a pause.

My cheeks start to warm, but the pit of my stomach pulls down in a sickening way.

"And?" Lowell asks.

I frown. "I said I don't have sex with clients for magic."

Lowell tilts his head. "Huh."

"What?"

"Just…" Lowell trails off before starting again. "Your first reaction to an attractive man wanting to have sex with you is to treat it like prostitution."

"Well—sexy *client*… and the way he made it out, the reason I should say yes was for the magic."

I stumble over my words. Why am I stumbling?

"When did you start caring so much about that? I know you don't do things in exchange for magic, but you used to jump into orgies just for fun. That it contributes funds to the family business just made it better."

He isn't wrong. I've never felt inhibited about sex. It never occurred to me to feel that way before the Jackson incident.

Lowell keeps talking. "And I know I'm not supposed to notice anything about your sex exploits, because family and all, but you haven't participated in anything for a long time. Like longer than you've ever gone without before."

My cheeks burn and embarrassment swallows me whole. Katherine, Wanda, and now Lowell, has everyone noticed my abrupt celibacy?

Lowell persists. "People are worried about you, Rose. I field inquiries a few times a week about how you're doing. Katherine just asked if she should get a friend of hers to curse the guy with impotence. Actually, you should check in with her anyway. I don't trust that she hasn't already done something. *Not that I'd lose sleep over that.*"

The last of Lowell's words end on a mutter and I'm torn between the lasting burn of humiliation and a heartwarming laugh. It would seem that yes, everyone has noticed.

"We've all been giving you space, but we still worry that you've been cutting yourself off from the community," he says.

"Oh," I stall.

It's not like I've completely cut myself off from the world. Jared and Lowell still come over for movie night every week and I talk to every person who approaches me at the bathhouse but… I can see what he means. It's been mostly me going through the motions. Not wanting to dive into intimacy. Not wanting to match with my favorite tools.

"I haven't felt like participating lately." And I really, really haven't.

"And that your sudden drop in libido coincided with the Jackson incident."

The Jackson incident. We don't even call it a relationship, or a breakup, because I was the only one to think it was a relationship.

"I don't know how much I want to talk about my libido with you," I say the words, but they lack any feeling.

Lowell's laugh is small. "Believe me, I don't want to meditate about it or anything. Just pointing out observations. And hey, if this Gideon guy does nothing for you or came off like an asshole, I'd say you're right to reject him. I wasn't there for the conversation. I just watched his backside as he left."

I cough a laugh, but my mind chews on that. Because Gideon did do something for me. Lots of things. He's actually the first person to pique my interest since everything fell apart.

"You're saying I should consider it?"

Lowell ponders for a second. "I'm saying I don't know why you're not."

"It's unprofessional?"

And gets dangerously close to making me feel *cheap*. Again.

But that isn't me. Rose Love is not a woman who is cheap or should be concerned with feeling cheap based on one bad interaction with one man, months ago. Sex doesn't cheapen people.

Lowell's disbelief has me smiling for real.

"Rose, this is a place without judgment around sex. Unprofessional and wrong in our sphere is something egregious, like selling client information or blackmail. Not something like having sex with a client because they're hot." He makes a sound and waves his hands in exasperation. "Plus, he isn't really your client anyway, you aren't finding a match for him."

There's a beat of silence. The fact of the matter is….

"You're right." My admission is small.

Lowell gasps dramatically and I poke him in the side.

"Maybe I'll consider it."

If I consider it because I'm attracted to Gideon, intrigued by him as a person, or because it staves off my very real issue of not being able to matchmake, well, that's my business.

Later I sit at my desk, the stark white card staring at me alongside my stationery. Worries whir through me. Worries about the business, matching, my personal happiness. My mind keeps sticking on the way Gideon's eyes darkened with want, and how my heart raced from the thrill of it.

Something needs to change.

I pick up the card.

CHAPTER 6

 GIDEON

Excitement surges through my veins as I enter the coffee shop. The very coffee shop I spent my morning in, though no one will recognize me. My creature masks my presence as a natural instinct. The barista who takes my order merely forgets my existence after serving me.

Rose asked for this meeting. Her call came much earlier than I figured it would with how angry she had been with my offer. Mace had only just returned me to this city after teleporting me to the bank that safeguards some of the shiny things I've collected over the years.

Courting calls for gifts, after all.

And the demon did want to be helpful.

I have a mental shout of triumph when I see that Rose has already taken a seat, but outwardly frown that she's not only ordered already, but she's ordered for me. I have to bite back the dominant urge to provide for this woman. It's instinct, but instinct won't win over strategy.

"I'm willing to meet, to talk this over, but everything is going to be according to my terms." Those had been her exact words on the phone. I swore to her that she would be the one to navigate our course and I need to stand by that.

Rose sees me and her eyes light up in interest even as her hands begin to fidget with her mug. I will bite back as many urges as needed for this opportunity.

"You already ordered for me."

Rose nods coolly.

"It's a latte." She narrows her eyes at me, biting her lip in indecision. "I should have ordered you black coffee."

I smile at her divining my coffee preference. "This is fine, but I'll admit I'm more curious about what we came to discuss."

Rose blushes, and I want to scrape my teeth over the heated skin. *Patience, Gideon.*

"Yes, we're discussing a possible agreement between us," Rose says primly. She turns the coffee mug in her hands, stalling. The thin silver rings that decorate her fingers have tiny moons and stars that tap against the ceramic.

"You wanted to talk about your terms," I start, eating up every reaction, every graceful motion.

Rose nods. "I'm open to the option of us being intimate for three sessions, but I have stipulations."

Three nights to convince this woman to be my mate. A challenge surely, but not impossible.

"What are your stipulations?"

"I want to get to know you first." Rose's words are strong, as if she expects me to reject them.

It's for the best that my little witch gets to know me. For her to trust me when I do ask her to commit her life to me.

"How would you like to get to know me? I'll answer whatever question you ask…"

This surprises Rose and I take note of that. I've been told that I can be cryptic and uncommunicative, but I don't want that for our relationship.

I continue, "Or do you mean that we should go on dates?"

"Um, I guess dates were what I had in mind. I do have questions, but I don't want to be rude," she hedges.

Ah, there are many things the paranormal community don't bring up in common conversation. Most likely she wants to know if I'm willing to talk about what kind of paranormal I am. The practice of not asking is a hold out from the time that rarer paranormal beings were hunted or enslaved by nefarious parties on a large scale.

Theoretically, the creation of the Council prevents modern day slavery from happening, but the Council is only populated with the most common paranormal beings, shifters and witches. When other paranormal beings go missing there's still an official process around it but there is a lack of confidence that it's treated as urgently as those who can contact Council officials through connections.

So, the practice of not asking about the type of paranormal someone is, persists.

"I will consider nothing you ask as being rude. It's only fair for you to know everything you desire to know before we are intimate," I say.

Rose's breath catches at the word *intimate*, and I clench my fists in my lap under the table, resisting the urge to reach toward her. I want her in my lap for this discussion, but we're in public, and it's hardly a good negotiation practice.

Rose purses her lips. "I want it agreed that either of us can break this agreement without repercussions."

My muscles tense, but I suppress my creature's rejection.

"Of course." Another fair term even if I hate it.

Rose's shoulders drop like she's surprised I haven't objected to any of her terms. Little does she know that

I'd give her anything she'd ask for. I sip the frothy latte to give her time to decide what comes next. It only takes my determined little witch a moment before she holds out her hand for a formal handshake to seal the deal.

"That's a more family-friendly way to seal the agreement than I figured we'd do," I tease, but grasp her small hand in mine.

I savor the heat of the first real skin contact with my mate. I stroke my thumb over hers until she breaks the handshake, squeezing her hand as if I've given her a shock.

She gives me a tiny smile. "Well, we are in public."

"We are. The better to get to know you without being consumed with lust." My words are light but the rustle of fabric from Rose pressing her thighs together tells me I'm not the only one affected by the other's presence. The scent of her skin at this distance has had me half hard during our discussion. Only the need to strategize has doused my body's need to a reasonable level.

"So, when did you realize you wanted to be a matchmaker?"

I start the get-to-know-you part of the evening with purpose. I don't want any delays in this, but I'll let Rose stop if she desires more time. More space.

"Oh, you want to—I mean of course you'd want to also get to know me… um, I've always wanted to match people." Rose stops, as if surprised by her own answer before continuing, "I'd watch my great-grandmother Bitsy match people and it fascinated me. It seemed like such a simple thing that made people so happy…"

My mate's face goes soft at that.

"Did she teach you?" I ask.

"In a way. Part of matching has always come easy to me. I've always been able to read how compatible a match will be—" Rose frowns and breaks off.

The urge to prod, to expose every aspect of this woman's life, is strong but I restrain myself. *Slow and steady, Gideon.*

"What about you? Your business card said you're a treasure hunter. What does that mean exactly?"

"Someone wants to find something; they call me, and I hunt it down for them."

Rose's mouth twists. "So, say I couldn't find my house keys."

A chuckle breaks from me at the playful note of her voice. "Sure, but it would cost you dearly."

"My house keys are very dear to me."

I lean forward, my hand stroking hers until she turns it palm up for me. The action is slow, a little hesitant until I touch her sensitive palm.

"Well, in that case. I'd invest myself fully in methodically looking through your life." I trace the lines on her palm with my thumb, making circles over the delicate veins of her wrist. "Explore every bit of it. Slowly hunt through every aspect that makes you the person you are. Until, I find your... keys."

Rose's inhale is reedy, and she blinks rapidly before narrowing her eyes.

"You're casting a spell on me," she whispers.

My sly smile doesn't seem to comfort her. "I'm not. I don't have that ability."

Rose's cheeks turn an endearing pink color.

"Oh, um, that brings up something I wanted to ask..." Discomfort lines her eyes and I want to chase it away, to bring back the glazed-eye look she'd given me from my small touches.

The pink of her face goes to red and my curiosity is fathomless.

"Yes?"

"What are you?" Her question comes out on a squeak.

I try hard not to laugh. We'd already cleared the air that asking this question is not rude, but a lifetime of paranormal polite conversation rules is a hard thing to depart from. Ridiculously, I have the urge to squirm. I never talk directly about my kind to someone I just met and I'm a little unsure of how Rose will react.

"Oh gods, I've offended you! I haven't been out in forever and I'm messing this up."

"No, you aren't messing anything up. I'm just not in a hurry for you to decide that this kind of agreement isn't for you." I wince because that doesn't sound good.

"Curiouser and curiouser." Rose lifts an eyebrow. "This talking directly about these matters is uncomfortable."

I give a hearty laugh. "I agree. I'm discovering I've never really answered that question. People either know or find out, it's rare that I tell anyone directly."

"Well, I know you must be ancient," she says.

"Positively." I take a breath. "Have you ever heard of a kraken?"

CHAPTER 7

ROSE

The vase on display is unique. Some pottery rescued from the bottom of the sea. But I'm not really seeing it. I stare through the glass and let my mind reel.

"Have you ever heard of a kraken?"

"When you say kraken, we are talking about the giant octopus that sinks ships?" I ask, just in case I'm mistaken.

Gideon nods and his ease bleeds away. I put up a finger. "Just give me a minute."

The minute had turned into two of me silently blinking, lost in thought. Gideon had suggested that we move our date to the exhibit of the local history museum where he knew a curator. The museum has an After Dark event going on, it's called Mixers with Mummies or something like that. I wanted a date and Gideon delivered.

The walk over, the line for tickets, and now the exhibit itself is a fuzzy blur because I can't stop my thoughts from turning over in my mind.

I've met a large variety of paranormal beings. I'm a witch, all my family are witches, but the bathhouse caters to everyone. I've even met more than my fair share of rare paranormal beings: demons, gargoyles, djinn, nymphs, shifters of all kinds, and just this morning, a harpy.

But never a paranormal of mythic proportions like a *kraken*.

I blink at the vase. What does this mean for sex? Is this the *undesirable* thing Gideon mentioned before? Does he have to have sex as an actual kraken? So many questions, all I have to do is ask. Just open my mouth and ask the man who has let my silence drag on the entire date.

There is a press at the small of my back. Gideon's hand. He's kept from touching me after the revelation, until now. It's as if he can't keep from soothing me. The action is so courteous that it helps loosen my tongue.

"I'm sorry I've been quiet," I whisper, head full of thoughts of whether I find tentacles desirable or not. How would that even work?

Gideon shrugs stiffly. "It's a lot to take in at once."

I don't mean to, but my choked laugh escapes me. When Gideon just blinks at me, I realize he doesn't hear the innuendo of his words or know the track of my thoughts.

"So, uh, tentacles, huh?" I ask.

I'm fascinated by the reddening of the tops of Gideon's cheekbones.

"Maybe we shouldn't talk about this here."

I may have lost my matching *mojo* as Lowell calls it, but I'm experienced enough to tell when a man is aroused. The way his breathing catches and one very obvious signal.

I let my gaze fall downward and catch the outline of Gideon's erection and take note that the form he currently wears isn't completely different than a human.

I shouldn't tease him. Not when I'm not sure where this is going. When I'm not sure that I won't call off this whole business. But it's hard to resist. Too hard.

"Are those in the undesirable category, or the desirable category?"

Gideon exhales slowly. He glares at me but the look has no sharp edges. He's not angry, but challenging.

"Like other shifter types, partial shifting during sex is incredibly pleasurable for my kind."

Now I'm the one with the burning face. The heat doesn't stop at my face though, my body is waking up with a vengeance after an ice age.

"Oh." I breathe.

Of course I know that little sex secret about shifter types. It's generally a taboo thing, but the bathhouse is a place of no judgment. Many shifters enjoy sprouting fangs or some extra fur, let their beast take over a little bit. It's hot to watch and experience.

"The question is whether that would be desirable to you." Gideon's voice is playful. "I can keep my parts to myself if you hate the idea."

Tentacles.

"I'm not saying no." Because I'm not. Interest makes my blush worse. "But I also just don't know."

I don't want to get his hopes up and then dislike it.

Gideon just nods and his fingers stroke designs on my lower back. "We can play it by ear."

"I'm assuming these are size appropriate tentacles and not bringing-down-a-ship tentacles?"

Gideon laughs. It's a nice laugh, just as I noticed in the coffee shop, deep with a husky quality that hints at disuse.

"Unless your other form is just the size of a regular cephalopod and the tales of wrecking ships are an exaggeration." Now that I've gotten over my shock, I have so many questions.

"My other form is of ship-wrecking size and if we explore that in our intimacy you won't have to worry about that scale. I am more magic than anything else, so everything will be size appropriate for the function."

The function of fucking. The magic thing makes sense with how magic exudes from him. Filling every space he enters. And now I'm blushing again. The heat is welcome though. This is fun.

To distract myself from how easy our interactions are, I stroll to the next exhibit. The display text reads that the assortment of patina-covered coins on display were pulled from a Spanish ship that wrecked in the 1600s.

I tilt my head at Gideon. "Something you need to confess to me? Shipwrecks are your thing."

He reads the text and I watch his mouth move with the words.

"Perhaps going to a museum for a date was a mistake." His tone is grave.

A flash of shock then disbelief moves through me. "What? No way—"

I cut off when Gideon's arm wraps around me and pulls me in, I get the impression that getting him to let me go again will be a struggle. The press of his body against mine as his chest shakes with a silent laugh is too nice to consider escaping.

He's joking.

"Some parts of my life are a little fuzzy. Times throughout history where I've had more power than brains. So, it could have been."

I gape at him.

Gideon's face cracks into a smile. "But most likely not."

I laugh in relief, but it's starting to dawn on me just how long Gideon has been alive.

"How *old* are you?" The question bubbles out of me before I think about politeness. I try to switch it with one that would be less rude. "Are there many of your kind?"

"Too old."

I tilt my head, silently requesting more and Gideon tightens his hold around me.

"To be honest, no one knows where kraken came from. Not even the kraken." Gideon's voice takes on the cadence of telling a story as if it didn't include his own origins. "A handful of us just appeared, we have no memory that includes anything other than being in the sea. Eventually times changed, we changed, until some of us could leave Mother Ocean, take on a form that allows us to exist in a modern world."

Like a magical evolution. Sea monsters taking human shape in a changing world.

"Do you keep in touch with others of your kind?"

Gideon blinks and shakes his head.

"No. The last one I crossed paths with was a few hundred years ago. He told me the others were either dead or sleeping."

"Sleeping?"

"When a creature lives for so long, ennui is the main cause of death. I've known ancient dragons who gave up, buried themselves deep in caverns, and slowly transitioned to rock. I imagine my kind do something similar, hiding themselves away in the deepest parts of the ocean, never to surface again."

Gideon's eyes are on the coins, but his voice sounds as if it's leagues away even as his arms are tight around me.

It sounds sad. As if the creatures of old are wrapped in loneliness. No family, no shared history. Worry grips me with tiny claws. It's ridiculous to worry about a man I just met, a powerful monster, but worry never follows logic.

The worry tells me how much I already like Gideon.

"How do you keep from getting that way? Losing the will to go on?"

Gideon blinks and turns his face to mine. His eyes trace lines over my face, as if he's devouring the look of me before settling on my lips and my breath stutters. Gideon's focus breaks and he loosens his hold on me.

The absence of the squeeze leaves me unmoored and I take his hand, not letting myself analyze the affectionate gesture. Gideon's eyebrows raise in surprise before giving my hand a squeeze and answering my question.

"My job is actually a big part. Hunting is something that appeals to my creature side. That the jobs I take on are for items considered precious, helps." His smile is small. "I'm a greedy beast that likes shiny objects."

That surprises a laugh from me.

Gideon continues, "Mostly, I just focus on the here and now. And I have friends."

I open my mouth to ask when I can meet his friends but snap it shut and pull my hand away. Gideon's brow furrows, but he lets me go.

"You stay present," I say, trying to keep myself from being pulled in.

I won't be meeting Gideon's friends. This *date*, this get-to-know-you, is about informing me if I want to enter into a short sexual interlude with this man. This is not the start of a relationship. This is not a match.

Those things aren't meant for me. Not in this case anyway. Gideon was clear about what he wanted when he approached me for an agreement centering around the bathhouse.

I can't let myself get attached to this man. Especially if he doesn't have soul threads. Compatibility is one thing, but in order to actually mate, to share a soul bond, soul threads are needed. Without a soul bond, there really isn't a future between a witch and an immortal.

I move to the next items on display.

Forcing my mind on facts I need to mention, to talk about, in order to know if this sexual interlude is possible.

"I've had a lot of sexual partners. Like, a lot." I force out the words. They taste bitter. I've never had to treat this like a dirty secret before. That I feel like it's necessary after the Jackson incident is telling. It strums dregs of anger and hurt in me.

Gideon's brows draw together in confusion.

"Your means and opportunity are rather phenomenal so that isn't really a surprise…" His words trail off as if he's trying to figure out why I'm telling him this.

"Does it bother you?"

Gideon doesn't respond right away and my shoulders tense. I glance back at him and his head tilts in a curious way.

"Why would it? I haven't lived a celibate life, Rose."

My sigh is harsh, my relief acrid rather than sweet.

"It bothers some people." Some people would use the term *used goods*.

"The wrong people." The glower on Gideon's face has something softening in my chest.

"Yeah, the wrong people," I mutter, but I feel incrementally lighter.

"Do you want to talk about it?"

The sound that comes out of my mouth is curt.

"No."

Gideon's hand presses against my lower back again. The gesture is a comforting one, a coaxing one. When his hand trails and grips my waist, I sigh.

"Me spilling all of my vulnerabilities to a man I just met sounds like a bad date for you." It's an evasion. I don't need to talk about my issues with a man I'm only interested in for sex. But some small part of me, the part that felt lighter at Gideon's glowering face, wants to talk about it.

Gideon leans his face near my ear, as if to whisper a secret, but the breath on my neck from his words has shivers running down my spine.

"I want nothing more than every single thing about you, Rose. I want you vulnerable to me."

The closeness of his mouth to my neck brings to mind a predator and his prey. I like the sensation that races through me. It's going to be hard to remember that this is only about sex when he says things like that.

"Am I the only one that's going to be vulnerable then? Maybe you should tell me your weak spots, then we'd be fair."

Gideon stops and distances himself slightly in a way that indicates that he does have weak spots. Secrets that can flay him open just like my memories flay me.

Regret stabs me. I'd only been teasing.

"No—that's not fair. I'm the one to bring up my past issues," I say.

"You may have learned this in time, but I'll give you anything you desire of me, little witch. Whatever deep secrets I hold are already yours."

My brain stumbles. Gideon can't actually mean that.

Gideon stares at the exhibit in front of us, not seeming to see it.

"And it's probably something that should be discussed before we are intimate anyway."

I wait, trapped by curiosity.

"I've always wanted to be a father. To have young." His confession tears through him. "But, like most immortals, krakens have never been known to breed."

"Oh, Gideon." My heart bleeds at the stricken look in his eyes before he buries it.

Gideon sighs. "Don't bother yourself with old wounds, little witch. I've fostered many foundlings in my time but the idea of raising my own flesh and blood, something I won't outlive… it's an ever-present ache. But—" Gideon takes a breath and gives me a teasing look. "It doesn't mean it will never happen, or that I can't practice."

I cough at the light tease.

He sobers. "We'll still need to use some form of contraceptive when we're together though. So that you're protected."

"I'm covered." I gesture to my neck. One of my necklaces is a simple medallion customized with a rose quartz; the spell it holds is set into the very metal to give the most security and strength. The charm prevents pregnancy and had been a gift from my female relatives when I'd started menstruating. A tradition with most witch families.

Sometime during our exchange, my heart and mind had made a verdict. I want to be intimate with this man. The care he takes in every interaction, how much I'm enjoying our soft banter, and my body's reaction. Gideon is exactly who I want to break my sexual fast with.

Gideon eyes the medallion and raises his hand to it; his smile is soft as his finger brushes the pink quartz. The action feels almost as naked as this conversation.

Shiny things. Like when I see a pretty paper that I want to add to my collection. The similarity of that is a connection. An indication that we understand each other, at least a small amount.

That sensation and Gideon's revelation are making it difficult to reply. I have no words for this moment except the ones he asked of me. A vulnerability.

"In all my time matchmaking, out of the hundreds of matches I've made, I've only made five or so perfect matches. People that are a hundred percent compatible. Soul mates. Whatever term you want to ascribe them." My throat swells and I pause. Trying to get through this. Give Gideon a little bit of my pain to make up for the pain he gave me. How intimate of an action, sharing wounds.

"I found mine a few months ago."

Gideon's body tenses beside me.

"And after a week or so, he rejected me."

It sounds so simple when I say it out loud. So clean. So clinical.

It doesn't include how happy I was to find the person who I believed to be my other half. Matching people who are a hundred percent compatible is supposed to be like hitting the lottery. The matches I'd seen and made were like witnessing moments of love at first sight. My own parents were considered a perfect match by my grandmother. I expected to start a life similar to theirs, falling in love, raising the next generation of Love witches.

The clinical words don't include the confusion I experienced from the way Jackson and my relationship went. The few times we were intimate and how the things he said still haunt me.

It doesn't include the devastation of being rejected. Because of who I am, what I do, what I've done.

I'd met my perfect match and he told me I was an easy enough fuck, but not someone he could bring home to his parents. The Love Bathhouse is well known after all. His family would never want to be aligned to such an establishment.

I had been so sure, so hopeful, I invested everything of myself, expecting this mythical perfect match to catch me and ended up dashed upon the rocks instead.

"I'm a bad person." Gideon's matter-of-fact words break me from my misery.

"What?"

Gideon gives me a smile that's all teeth. "I want to find this man and break his back for hurting you. At the same time, if he hadn't, I'd have broken his back to get to you."

Something about the viciousness of his words, the primal quality of them, has my soul stilling. On one side, seeing the beast Gideon spoke about slip through is terrifying, on the other I'm confusingly comforted about it. This is a creature that wouldn't let a woman it wanted go.

It's wrong.

But it soothes my torn apart heart.

While Jackson was more concerned about how it would look to marry a witch that works at a sex bathhouse, this creature might not even let me go if I wanted it to. If he wanted to keep me, that is.

I swallow.

"If you keep saying things like that, I'm going to start believing them."

CHAPTER 8

GIDEON

The street is wet from the drizzling rain. The light of streetlights reflects off the puddles in an eerie way. This is my favorite type of air. I can smell the ocean even though we're a good city away from the coast.

If I were alone, I'd let the tiny drops hit my face and revel in the moment that air becomes water. Instead, I hold an umbrella and Rose huddles into me. Her warmth at my side is better than enjoying the rain.

I thought I had pushed too hard. Shown too much of my hand when my creature surfaced, prodded by absolute jealousy from the story of Rose's ex.

But Rose had just looked at me, parting her lips in that distracting way of hers, and said she'd seen enough mummies for the night. That had been after her confusing statement about starting to believe the things I say. As if it was a threat.

I sense no disgust from her. No signals that she doesn't welcome my presence.

It's still a struggle to keep the creature at bay when the pain echoes from her so sharply. Maybe I should participate in a different kind of hunt soon. I'd only need to find the man's name. I can't ask Rose though, she'd see through any ploy now that she's seen me slip. Heard the threat on my tongue.

Or maybe I should focus on my courting strategy. The way Rose had spoken of a relationship and matches made it sound as if they are things she no longer wants.

Yes. This is where I need to focus, not on the possibility of crushing a man who'd put that shattered look in Rose's eyes.

Focus.

"When can I see you again?" I ask.

Rose starts at the sound of my voice. "You're seeing me right now."

"Ah, but I'd like to know when I can take you on a date again. Maybe somewhere that isn't littered with objects from my possible crimes."

Rose's laugh is light.

"I was just thinking we could head over to the bathhouse. Take a private room for the night," she says.

Confusion and a roaring arousal compete for mental power. I did notice that we were walking in the direction of the bathhouse, but I'd discounted the observation since Rose's home is also this way. A fact that she isn't aware I know. Yet.

"I thought you wanted to get to know me?" I ask.

"I have gotten to know you, Gideon Strand. I know that you were calm and collected as I came around to the idea of what you are. I know that you aren't going to shame me for my prior sexual experience, and I know I'm attracted to you."

We're one block away from the bathhouse now. I'm trying to think fast. To keep from blundering.

"I thought you wanted to take your time. Learn to trust me."

Rose shrugs. "I trust you with my body and that is what our agreement is about."

Fuck.

The plan had been to physically seduce my mate and that the rest would naturally flow from there. But now that I know Rose, know how she has been hurt in the past, this feels too soon. I should woo her first.

Rose deserves to be wooed.

"Unless you've changed your mind." There's a waver in her voice that I want to destroy.

I've lost this battle. I can't reject Rose offering her body just because I want her heart and mind too.

"No, Rose. I won't ever change my mind."

CHAPTER 9

ROSE

I close the door of our private room before locking it.

I won't ever change my mind. The fervor in which he spoke those words is significant, but what does he mean? He won't change his mind about our agreement? It didn't sound like he was talking about a short interlude, it sounded… profound. But that doesn't make sense.

Stop it, Rose. I need to take his words at face value. I can't afford the mental spirals that come from trying to find meaning that may or may not be there.

Being in one of the bathhouse rooms again is a comfort I didn't know I missed. The air is humid and warm. A mix of spicy scents permeate the space. The room is decorated with geometric patterns in the tile work like the lobby. There's a portion that's padded, floor to walls, with bedding. The other side of the room has a deep bathing pool, better for four people max.

I have a ridiculous memory of a time we tried to fit eight. So many of my good memories come from the bathhouse but I haven't let myself ponder on them recently. Every time a memory surfaces is like a tiny razor, cutting. After Jackson, all the happy memories are now each a reason why he didn't want me.

Maybe being in this space, letting myself remember who I am, will wash away the taint of rejection.

I've lived my life full of fun and family duty. There is no shame in being sexually promiscuous with consenting adults.

Frustration eats at me. This is my second favorite private room because I used my favorite room with Jackson. Because it was special to me. That room has a completely pink and gold color scheme with my favorite mosaic design, roses. This room is still beautiful, with a main theme of navy, and a mosaic design of a night sky with silver and gold stars.

I will not let that asshole ruin anything else for me.

Determination has me roughly removing my clothes. My jeans scrape my skin as I tug them off. I toss my items in some provided baskets that keep things from getting wet. The whole room can become a splash hazard at the best of times. I don't even look at Gideon until I'm naked.

The man is motionless, just taking in the expanse of my body with dark eyes. There is no chill in the room, but goose bumps raise on my skin.

"You're overdressed," I say.

"Perhaps I want you to be the one to take off my clothes."

Gideon looks so formidable standing there. His height, wide shoulders, and stern bearing has my conviction faltering. He's just so much.

I want to cover my bareness in the face of the hunter in front of me. What was I thinking?

"I-I need to light the candles."

I turn from Gideon and the sound of rustling cloth fills the room as my bare feet take me over the smoothed tile floor to the altar. It isn't really an official altar, but a streamlined version. All the spells are already set into the room. Some of the oldest ones are in the tilework itself but we've added newer ones in gold paint on the marble.

All that's needed to start our session is to light the candles together. It serves as a contract of sorts. To light the candle is to agree to the draining of the magic produced by our acts.

I try to center myself with the starting of the ritual. I sort through the cabinet and bring out three white pillar candles that I arrange on a wax-covered stand. Using a long match, I start with the candle at the end of the line.

The flame of the match wavers. My hand shakes with nerves. The wick of the candle catches, and I stop.

I curse my awkwardness. I've started this ritual too soon. Damn nerves.

Gideon needs to light the candle on the other side of the middle candle next. I turn and he's there. Every part of him on display.

The lit match is forgotten as I get my first visual of this man who will soon be inside me. I'd known his shoulders were broad, that his waist tapered attractively in his dress clothes. But with no coverings, the planes and strength of his body stands in relief. Skin demarcated by dips and bulges of flesh that I want to grip between my teeth.

And that's without looking at his cock. My eyes skate over that part, wanting to save that moment for later, though I can tell he's already hard. My lower body feels empty, hungry, needy.

His appearance is only one side of the coin. A beautiful, shiny side of the coin but the flip side is darker, more beguiling. It's the strums of power that echo in my stomach. His mere stance and pithy distance make my thighs want to squeeze together.

My numb fingers almost drop the match and Gideon moves quickly. His hot hand wraps around mine, taking the burning match. The action is graceful and brings his bulk right up against me. Our skin touches and I'm distracted for a moment with the lovely brush of his texture. The roughness of his skin and wiry hair against my hip, his chest against my arm, the drag of the fingers of his free hand up my back.

This man is a seduction. A heavy weight pulling me under the surf to the very depths, where there is no breath or time. I can't make myself struggle. I'd give up my breath to have this dangerous man.

"Rose, what am I doing?"

I blink in confusion. *What is he doing?* What a good question. Why is he here with me when he could get any woman he wants? Why a matchmaker witch going through a crisis of confidence?

"Rose, the match is still burning." Gideon's voice sounds teasing but his eyes crinkle in concern.

"Oh! Uh, light that candle. Then we light the middle one and blow out the match together."

Gideon's steady hand lights his candle and tentatively I wrap my small hand around his and we light the last candle before slowly bringing up the match between us and blowing it out. There's a crackle of static to the air that signifies the ritual has been completed.

Anticipation rolls through me from the action, hot and coaxing.

Gideon's face is soft, and he leans in as if to kiss me. Him suddenly being so close, so final, has fear driving my stomach into my throat; shattering the hot feelings that had flowed so freely. I turn my head, dodging the kiss and quickly dispose of the blackened match.

I castigate myself for the retreat. How is this going to happen if I can't even let myself be kissed?

I want to be kissed, to be touched.

Gideon allows me to turn away but catches my hand. The action isn't forceful, it's comforting. Bitterness rises in my throat. I shouldn't need this special handling.

"You're nervous." Gideon's words aren't a question.

I'm trembling.

I force out a breath.

"It feels like it's been a long time since I've last done this." And that didn't end well.

Gideon's movements are slow, incrementally so. He gives me time to move away as he comes up behind me. His presence there lets me watch the flickering candles, spelled to burn slowly, instead of having to face him.

"May I touch you?"

Gideon doesn't sound as if it's an inconvenience to have to ask and that diminishes some of my fears. Fears that I'm suddenly too high maintenance. This man is a good man to end my dry spell with. An excellent sexual partner if the careful way he beguiles me is to be a judge. A partner that I'm trying to not get attached to.

I push down my doubts and nerves, making myself stand still and nod.

I'm rewarded with Gideon's large hands trailing up my back. He softly runs his calluses over my skin before rubbing his thumbs into the muscles of my upper back.

I melt. It's slow at first, my muscles stiff with anxiety and swirling worry, but the persistent touches pull the knots out, making me pliable.

Gideon's voice keeps my legs from going to liquid, but only just.

"We don't have to do this now. Or even at all. If you want to go back to going on dates, I was thinking a picnic tomorrow would be nice. If it ever stops raining here."

I breathe a laugh at that. "I want to do this. I need to."

Gideon hums and I think he might understand the things I'm not saying. That I need to prove to myself that I can still do this.

His hands lay flat on my back, and I feel the brush of his lips on my shoulder. The small gesture holds an affection. Confusion has my throat thickening.

"Bathe with me, Rose."

Gideon slides his hands away but takes ahold of mine again. I let him pull me toward the bathing pool. I haven't used the pools since everything happened. I work in a bathhouse and haven't even soaked innocently in the restorative water in months. My anger fires all over again, but I suppress it. The time of abstinence is over. In all senses.

And a hot soak sounds wonderful.

Gideon slowly enters the pool, using the submerged steps. I stop to pull my curls into a passable topknot. Now that his forbidding gaze isn't trapping me, my eyes travel over the muscles of his back and ass. The man has a ranginess to him that I can appreciate. Long limbs and muscles that are lean and hard. And so very bitable.

Since when have you been obsessed with biting, Rose?
Since Gideon, it seems.

The bathing pools are deep and delightfully hot. Gideon looks back at me with surprise when the water goes up to his upper chest with him standing.

I smile at him but stay on the shallower side, enjoying the sensation of hot water enveloping me. The comfort of it all is familiar, a deep soothing breath.

"The benches are at different heights to accommodate different body types." I gesture toward the benches.

Gideon dunks his head. The water lovingly runs down his face and hair when he surfaces. Buoyed, his movements become more fluid and easy. Like he's at home, and I guess he is.

"Is this your natural habitat?" I tease.

"This is much warmer than my natural habitat, but the company here is much better." Gideon's delight is infectious. "I feel the spells of this place. Your family has really done something marvelous here."

A warm glow fills my chest. I'm proud of this bathhouse but hearing the happiness and awe in Gideon's voice makes that pride shine brighter. A light while I stumble in the dark.

Gideon runs a finger over the runes carved into the rim of the pink crystal bathing pool. Practical spells guaranteeing the heat of the water and cleanliness. Spells for happiness and good health.

"Rose quartz?"

"Yes." I move closer to him as if to take a closer look. Our arms brush. "It's actually my namesake. We use it in a lot of the bathing pools. It has a lot of magical uses as well as being called the 'love' stone. How could the Love family possibly resist?"

"I'm glad you didn't resist. The stone hums, like it's alive, it's a nice addition." Gideon's eyes are on me now. The red of my cheeks is obviously from the heat of the water and not from the way his eyes darken at my nearness.

Our long look is broken by the quick movement of Gideon's arm wrapping around my waist, and I'm pulled in as if I've been caught by a sea monster. I cry out, but my arms come down around his neck and my cry turns into a laugh.

Gideon sits on one of the benches that brings the water up to our necks. I straddle him in my captured state, too joyful to be awkward about his thick body being between my legs until I feel the throb of his erection against my thigh. I stiffen.

"Ignore that," Gideon says lazily.

I snort.

"You want me to ignore your cock? That will result in an interesting night."

"It has no sense of timing and timing is everything. So, ignore it." Gideon starts rubbing my back again. The heat of the water and the massage loosens the tight worry in my chest.

I sigh, giving into the skilled coaxing of this ancient creature. "You're too good at that."

The skin crinkles around Gideon's eyes.

"It's my pleasure to touch and taste every inch that you give to me. What do you like, little witch?"

The soft endearment in his rumbling voice is a caress. I squeeze my thighs around his body and try to think in coherent thoughts. Right. Ground rules.

"I don't have an interest in getting fucked in water. Lubrication is usually lacking for that."

Gideon raises an eyebrow. "We'll put that on the 'not today' list."

"How about the 'never' list."

"You might feel differently when it comes to tentacles."

My face flushes. "Oh."

"Which you can reject at any time. No questions asked. I care about your experience, Rose."

"Okay." I believe him.

"I asked you what you liked. I'll also take note of what you don't, but what do you want?"

The urge to hide my face is a writhing thing. To be anywhere but looking straight in Gideon's eyes. I do have a confession about what I want tonight, but admitting it is difficult. Gideon waits until my mouth opens.

"I don't want to have to ask for anything." My whisper is a broken, ugly thing. Showing this powerful man my jagged parts hurts in a way that I can't help but to hate. A blemish on the way I see myself.

I don't want to request something in good faith only to have my request met with disgust and disbelief. I don't want to be rejected.

I don't believe Gideon would do any of that, but I want a fantasy where my mind believes I'm completely safe. Maybe another time I'll be brave. I'll ask for what I want without fear because I deserve to be able to voice my wants in bed.

There's an intelligence in Gideon's eyes. As if he knows all my shameful feelings. With the slight sharpness in the air, I wonder if he's correctly deduced the reason for my request.

"I'll endeavor to make this a pleasurable experience without your direction. But, Rose, I need you to tell me if you don't like anything I do."

"Of course," I say, avoiding the searching look Gideon gives me.

"My pleasure is dependent on your enjoyment. I need to be able to trust that you'll tell me when you want me to stop."

It all sounds logical when he states it so plainly. I love logic, even when it's revealing.

"Of course." My words sound stronger, surer.

Gideon's body relaxes and it's a comfort that he cares so much. Maybe, just for tonight, I can pretend that this isn't just a short arrangement. Pretend that I get to keep him. My body responds to that fantasy more than I want to reflect on.

Tonight, I'll let myself forget that we're incompatible as mates.

My hands have a mind of their own as my fingers splay over Gideon's shoulders, but I stop them.

"Can I touch—"

"Yes," Gideon cuts me off and I giggle.

Gideon's face comes near mine, but he doesn't kiss me, merely presses his cheek to mine.

"I ache for your hands, little witch," he whispers in my ear and I shiver.

My fingers trace the muscles of Gideon's shoulders, up his neck, before running through his dark hair. The texture is silkier than I anticipated. So soft compared to the texture of my own curls.

"You ache for my hands here?" I tease and scratch softly at the back of his neck. The man smiles against my face.

"It's a good place to start."

Gideon places an opened-mouth kiss on my shoulder and the brief sensation of his tongue distracts me. I sigh.

"So many freckles," he murmurs, kissing my neck next.

Heat travels under my skin. Hotter than the bath, hot enough to burn away inhibitions.

"I like my freckles."

Gideon's hum tickles my skin and my hips tilt, my pussy aches from the slow drag of small touches my partner has been using to entice me. The brush of skin, the heat of his mouth, the massage of muscles. Each action pulls me down the spiral of attraction.

"Me too. Tiny flecks of gold that I want to sample one by one. Do you know what was going through my head when you angrily took off all of your clothes?"

Embarrassment fights with my arousal. "I wasn't angry. I was just… determined."

"Determined to fall on my cock? How romantic." Gideon parrots my words from earlier today. "Anyway, I admit I missed most of the expression on your face. I was distracted."

"What was going through your head?" I ask.

"That I found a treasure." Gideon's hands grip my ass and pull me against him, boosting me higher in the water. My breasts break the surface of the bathing pool. "A delightful treasure."

Gideon's head falls and he bestows small bites from my shoulder to my breasts. My nipples tighten and I moan when he sucks one into his mouth. My hips rock against his corded stomach, giving a small amount of relief to counteract the delicious sensation of Gideon's mouth drawing on my nipple, swirling his tongue around it.

A treasure. Can someone orgasm from praise alone?

He releases the sensitive tip

"And that your tits are amazing, but that thought may have come from lower than my mind." There's a growl to his voice now, and I use my grip in his hair to pull his head back to my breasts.

"Don't stop," I say, and I swear he smiles.

All thoughts about being called his treasure sail away when he draws hard on my nipple and pleasure pain has me crying out. Gideon's mouth softens but I babble at the absence.

"Noo, don't stop."

Gideon chuckles. "So you like your nipples a little tortured?"

"Not always, that just feels so good right now."

Gideon nips my breast before laving my nipple again and sucking. My core draws tighter with every pull and I whimper. Gideon must like the sounds because he continues to work me over before switching to the next breast.

I'm a mess, dissolving into sounds and sensation. I grind myself against whatever I can, but with Gideon's grip on my ass, the only hard flesh I'm grinding against is his torso.

I don't notice that we're moving until Gideon releases a nipple with a pop and carries me up the steps. I tighten my grip around his neck as the water runs off our bodies.

"What—"

"You said that getting fucked in water wasn't on your list, little witch." Gideon slowly lowers me to my feet. He grabs a towel and begins drying my body.

I should tell him that the bedding is spelled to absorb water, that this is unnecessary, but I don't. I like the methodical way he dries me, gently wiping the water from my skin, making sure to dry the calves of my legs. Kneeling to do so.

Gideon stops in his position and his eyes meet mine, filled with a dark hunger that belies the smooth smile on his face. His hands stroke up my legs to hold my hips before he presses his face against my pussy.

I jump at the contact, grabbing onto his shoulders. "You don't need to do—"

Gideon growls and I stop speaking when his tongue lightly licks up through my lips. My nails dig into his skin, and I'm trembling all over at the tiny tease.

Gideon pulls himself away and takes a breath. The air ghosts over my skin. He stands and picks me up again.

"I can walk." My voice is small, I love that he's carrying me. I let myself absorb the feeling of being held like this before Gideon kneels on the bedding and lays me down. I spread my legs, expectant, but he doesn't thrust himself into my empty core. He lays over me, making eye contact.

"I want to taste you." His voice is direct and stern. I squirm against his physical weight and the weight of his gaze. "You say I don't have to, but I'm asking, is this something you don't want, Rose?"

That's gross. Men don't enjoy doing that. Jackson's words were wrong. I've had so many partners who love performing oral sex. But the reaction of my perfect match when I asked for that is what stays in my head. It brought me low and hurt, still hurts.

That action doesn't even rank in deviancy compared to the other things I was going to ask of Jackson.

"I-I—" I break off, not knowing what to say and Gideon's face darkens in a fury I only caught sight of briefly at the museum. A mixture of anger and jealousy.

"I will do what I want, and you will tell me if you want me to stop. Correct, Rose?"

My stuttering mind eases with the command in Gideon's voice.

My answer comes out on a relieved sigh. "Yes."

CHAPTER 10

ROSE

Gideon moves down my body and I grab a plush pillow to prop myself up so I can watch. He drops soft kisses down on random freckles; it tickles and makes me want to grab his hair and direct him to where I ache for his mouth.

Gideon bites my inner thigh and I do grab his hair.

"Oh gods—" I break off on a moan from his hot mouth licking over my wet folds.

A deep groan rumbles from Gideon and he pushes my legs higher, spreads them wider before covering my pussy completely with his mouth. The man proceeds to eat me.

His tongue slides up to massage my clit and I pant. I've experienced oral many times in my life, but every person always does it a little different. Something about the intent way Gideon applies pressure with each lick, spirals my need out until it feels bigger than I can possibly take but not quite enough just yet. Gideon flattens his tongue and strokes my most sensitive parts and I gasp.

Gideon commits each action with determination. Driving me higher and higher until two fingers press deep inside me and he sucks on my clit.

The orgasm seems as if it comes out of nowhere, but I should know better. Every movement this man has made since entering my office has been strategic, carefully bringing us to the moment my vision goes white and my toes curl as I shatter on a desperate cry.

Gideon hooks his fingers harder inside me and my release pulses through my body again on a shudder.

I'm shaky and gasping but he doesn't give me any time to come down. Gideon surges up and conquers my mouth with his before I can escape.

I wouldn't have tried to.

The taste of him and me and the clash of his mouth on mine is an antidote to every doubting thought I've had. I wrap my legs around his waist and pull him in harder, demanding more.

Gideon curls his fingers again, and I squeeze around them with a moan before reaching down. I break our kiss.

"Not your fingers, I want your cock."

"Not yet." Gideon grits his teeth.

"Now!"

I wrap a hand around his cock and let myself finally look at it. *Oh, gods above, yes.*

It's thick and long, the skin mouthwateringly ruddy and Gideon laughs out a curse when I squeeze him. His hips jut forward eagerly.

"I knew there was a demanding little witch in there somewhere."

I freeze. He's right. I'm asking for something. It may seem like a small thing, but with how tongue-tied I've been up till now, triumph spears me. It makes me want something else spearing me.

I nip Gideon's lip and suck it with a groan. "Gideon."

He moans.

"I want to feel you inside me, Gideon, filling me up, replacing bad memories."

Gideon's mouth pulls into a snarl before he comes back to himself and glares at me. "Don't try and make me jealous just to get what you want, little witch."

I roll my hips toward him, running his cock through the wetness between my legs. Gideon's head drops at the slick-on-slick sensation.

"Then give me what I'm asking for."

I tilt my hips up and the head of him presses against my entrance. I look down, mesmerized. The wet head of his cock is a tease, so wide compared to where I want it. It's going to take work to take him. *Yes.*

"Slowly—"

I snort at that. "I can take you."

Gideon's eyes glitter. "Can you? Maybe I should make you do that sometime. Fuck yourself down on my cock, trying to make it fit instead of taking it slow and easy."

I arch my back, but two can play the dirty talk game.

"I like it when it hurts a little, when I have to stretch for you."

A shudder travels through Gideon and something primal shows through in the resulting stillness of his body.

"You're playing a dangerous game, little witch."

My toes curl at the way his voice sounds deeper and Gideon presses his cock into me. As predicted, it takes some force before my flesh gives to his. I moan at the stretch and almost don't hear Gideon speaking.

"When you let me partially shift, I want to do that to you. Fill you up completely, slowly stretch you until you can't take it anymore."

My face flushes past the point of embarrassment. Oh gods.

"More," I whisper.

Gideon continues, his cock so hard I ache.

It takes some patience and small thrusts, but he fits himself completely inside me. It's glorious. Gideon moans, skimming his lips up my neck to nip my ear.

"You're so tight around me. So hot. All mine."

My fantasy of keeping this man cheers.

"All yours," I echo. "But you need to move."

I mean the words to sound demanding, but they come out as a beg. Gideon begins moving inside me and it's perfection.

More perfect than any sex I'd had with my "perfect" match.

That single thought plucks at the haze of sensation of Gideon's rolling movements. I dig my heels into his ass.

"More. Harder. Please, Gideon."

Gideon narrows his eyes at me but straightens his arms and thrusts hard inside me. I make a sharp sound at the impact.

"Fuck, yes," I urge.

I groan into the next smack of his body against mine. The strokes are unforgiving, bruising almost. They're everything I've ever needed but poisonous doubts still latch on to me. That fucking is what I like best, that it's all I'm good for.

I squeeze my eyes shut and try to dispel the ugly thoughts full of rejection and malice.

Gideon's thrusts become softer, but he collars my throat with a hand and my eyes pop open.

"Stop thinking about anyone else, Rose." His tone borders on feral. "You're mine. I'm the one inside you."

I blink away the tears I didn't know were filling my eyes. Aroused beyond belief but furious that I can't stay out of my own head. That the doubts can reach me here.

It all makes me reckless. Desperate.

"Then fuck me like no one else does. Give me more of you, Gideon. Shift." *Claim me.* I can't bring myself to say that even in my fantasy state.

Gideon bares his teeth in a way that would be frightening if I wasn't so worked up and suddenly sensations change.

Things wrap around my thighs and immobilize me, keeping me spread as the unforgiving hardness of Gideon's cock changes. Softer, smoother, sliding into me and moving in a way that tickles before the pressure starts.

"Oh fuck fuck fuck."

It stops.

"Do you want to stop?" It costs Gideon to ask. Red flags his cheeks and his breathing is ragged.

I look down. The pale skin of Gideon's chest transitions darker at his lower body, where our bodies are flush against each other. Instead of legs, there are other limbs spiraling from him. Black, thick tentacles have wrapped around my thighs, restraining them. I test their strength by attempting to move my legs, but I can barely wiggle.

I'm well and truly caught. The detail I'd been avoiding until now, what I need to analyze, is that there's something inside me.

"Show me." My lips tremble at my request and *it* moves inside me, sliding out of me. The tentacle tip curls in front of me as if on display. Tilting my head, I reach out, poking the appendage and the tapered end curls around my finger, smearing wetness against my skin. "Is that one your cock?"

Gideon takes a breath, seeming as if he's trying to calm his arousal enough to have a conversation.

"Yes. Do you want an anatomy lesson about kraken right now?"

It sounds like a tease, but I think Gideon would do it if I asked.

"Can you... uh... do you release fluids from it?" Something from a documentary I saw forever ago has my mouth opening before I realize it. "Oh gods, it isn't detachable, is it?"

The man above me freezes, and his eyes widen before he clears his throat and looks down. My face is on fire and I continue to open my mouth.

"I just saw something on the Discovery Channel once—"

Gideon shakes his head back and forth, not looking at me. The tentacles holding my legs loosen and he lowers himself on top of me, hiding his face in the crook of my neck. His shoulders are moving, and it takes me longer than it should to realize he's laughing, uncontrollably.

"I don't think the question was that out there," I say as if I'm put out, but I'm having trouble not laughing as well.

If the circumstances were different, I'd probably take someone who had just been inside me laughing poorly. As it is, with the way Gideon clutches me, arms and a tentacle wrapping around my waist, closeness eases any insecurities that might plague me.

Instead—this complete loss of composure from such a forbidding individual is a prize that I'll hoard for the rest of my days. *A treasure.* My inner musings have a wry smile curving my lips.

"Just give me a second." Gideon speaks into my neck while making a gesture with his hand. But he continues to shake in poorly disguised laughter.

"You know, you could just say it's not."

Gideon shakes his head, but his arms tighten around me and he rolls onto his back, bringing me on top of him. I straddle him and sit up to see his face better. Gideon wipes his eyes, but the mirth is still there.

"You are a wonder," he says. There is no sarcasm flavoring his words. "For all of the worrying I did about your reaction I did not expect a question like that."

"You're the one that mentioned anatomy. I do know that there is a cephalopod that breaks off its penis and leaves it in the female."

Gideon is laughing again. There are more tears.

"Not this one, I assure you." Gideon's eyes are full of warmth and teasing.

I'm grateful for this break in the tension. It's nice to have a fun moment and laugh together. It's a component that I forgot about in my previous flings, sans the Jackson incident. The mere act of being comfortable with someone.

"So, this is part of you?" I ask as I take in the transition of his human form skin to the black tangle of suction cup limbs. I shrug. "I don't hate it. The texture was different... more squishy, and the pressure was something that took me by surprise."

Gideon's mouth quirks.

"Has anyone ever told you that you are remarkably adaptive and brave, Rose?"

I shake my head but freeze at the intense look on his face.

"Well, they should have. I called you a wonder and I mean it. Not many people would react to something like this so well."

My ears are starting to burn. I try to change the subject. "How were you making that pressure? The ends of you are so small."

A tentacle end comes into view and I watch as it swirls and twists on itself.

"So, you *were* stuffing me full." My thighs try to squeeze together at the thought of Gideon pushing my limits with something so foreign to me, but the bulk of him between my legs keeps them apart. "What do you like about it? Is that tentacle as sensitive as your cock?" I have so many questions, but I mostly just want to know how to make the man who called me a wonder feel good.

Gideon's smile is lazy, but I'm not fooled. His projection of ease disguises the primal part of him that I see in flashes. It's a lull, or a lure rather, until I'm wrapped up tight and can't get away. A little like I am now since a tentacle is still wrapped around my waist.

"Things feel *brighter* when I shift at least partially, more raw. And no, the tentacle doesn't have the same experience as my cock. I enjoy…" Gideon blushes a little and clears his throat. "I get off from the idea of seeing how much I can fit inside you."

You.

I stumble over that. Having a thing for stretching isn't an unusual kink, Gideon just has more organic means than others, but the *you*…. I test the waters.

"Do women usually enjoy that?"

Gideon doesn't respond right away. He lightly draws circles on my hips with his fingers.

"I haven't partially shifted with a woman before."

My eyes widen at that and Gideon's mouth purses.

"Sharing this with someone I don't know very well has never seemed worth the risk before."

"The risk?"

"It's difficult to know how some people will react to this." Gideon curls a tentacle in the air in emphasis. "And this is something personal to me. I didn't want to risk a bad reaction tainting it until I met you."

I understand that too well.

"And I somehow make you comfortable with exploring?"

"Yes." Gideon's eyes darken.

I want to ask "why?" but I stuff the question away. I can relate to not wanting to share certain desires. Maybe I'd tease him about there being a whole category of porn devoted to tentacles later.

The frank talk about sexual proclivities heats the air between us again. Tentacles wrap around my thighs again, keeping my legs spread. I bite my lip at the squeeze of the restraints, the slight tug outward they apply to my legs. The implied force quickens my heart and an ache blooms anew in me.

"My hands?" I ask, wiggling my fingers at the question. There's an answer I want, but we are so new as partners that I wonder what Gideon would want.

Waves of intention come off the man under me, and I squirm.

"Behind your back."

I draw my hands behind me only to feel the wrap of another tentacle trap them. Oh gods, can this man be any more perfect?

The tentacle that acts as Gideon's sex organ slides between my legs, more exploratory than claiming. It presses and rubs against my clit and I sigh. It feels like a giant tongue, stubbled with suckers.

"You do seem to be enjoying this," Gideon purrs. "But we can go back to regular sex if this is too much for you."

Gideon sounds teasing and slows the stimulation as if he's going to stop.

"I want to try this," I snap and rock my hips against that questing part of him. My lower body is still heavy with arousal and Gideon's gaze on my pussy has a whimper bubbling from my throat.

Gideon looks up at the sound. "So damn beautiful, Rose. Your pretty cunt is so wet and clasping. Does it need something?"

"Yes." I want to hide my face but I can't take my eyes off Gideon. "It's so empty."

"We can't have that."

Gideon's sex organ slides through my pussy again. A tease as the heat rises in my face.

"Please." My lips start trembling at the slide of his odd flesh inside me. The penetration is small but the taboo nature of watching something so odd disappear into my body, of feeling it move in me, has me panting out a moan.

"Does my witch need more?"

I nod and it starts. Gideon's tentacle coils before pushing in. I jump at the strange sensation of penetration. It's an easy glide at first before the width of the limb slows the process and the drag of him against my internal walls has me gasping, tightening on the flesh inside me. A pitched sound leaves my mouth before it turns into a moan.

A dull feeling of fullness starts to build in me. The small space of my body stretching with the press of him.

I try to keep from squirming as the pressure builds. My arms burn as I pull against my restrained wrists.

"Oh!" My breath shudders as a twist of the tentacle presses—hard—against my front interior wall.

"That's it."

Gideon uses his thumb to stroke small slow circles on my clit while the part he's trying to fit inside me continues to tunnel in. I'm so surrounded by sensations of him that his strokes pull a sensitivity from me that's almost painful.

"Oh Rose, you were wet before, but now you're positively soaking me." His voice coaxes me as my heart races.

I squeeze around him again helplessly. The stretch is immense, so different than using a hard object to push my boundaries. The flesh pressed inside me is soft but expands unforgivingly all at once.

I grunt; a cold sweat breaks out over my skin.

I want to take everything but—

"Stop." I gasp so softly that it's almost a surprise when Gideon's flesh inside me stills. "It's so tight. I don't know if I can... oh gods."

No more, I'm so full, no more can possibly fit.

Gideon keeps his thumb on my clit but runs his other hand over me, the sensation is so light, over my breasts, up and down my arm. It contrasts with the pressure inside me. Each soft touch, each pet, has my body wanting to lean into his touch.

"Shh, you're doing beautifully. So brave, little witch, look at how much you've taken."

I look down and throb at the sight of Gideon's thickness penetrating me.

"Oh fuck." My head tilts back and I try to keep my body from trying to fuck myself on him. Too full, too much, but my body still begs for a completion.

"Breathe, Rose."

We breathe together, and I meet Gideon's eyes. Lust and appreciation fill his face.

"That's it, little witch."

Now that my mind isn't completely spinning out of control with arousal, I bear down, knowing it'll help the stretch. Gideon's eyes glaze. I relax and Gideon and I groan in unison as his appendage slides in farther, as my body gives more to him.

"*Oh gods, oh gods, oh gods,*" I babble.

Gideon rubs faster on my clit as he sits up and catches a nipple in his mouth. I tense around him, gasping when the flesh inside me twists. The stretch combined with the drag of what must be the suckers on my internal walls has a cry leaving my lips.

"Gods, why does something so wrong feel so good?" The question is out of my mouth before I can think to temper it. I'm surprised by myself. Wrong and right are ideas that have no place in a consensual act like this one.

"Because you're my little deviant. Greedy for the way only I can fill you."

I tremble, reaching the edge of reason. Gideon's right, I'm insatiable, greedy, filthy, and just want more.

I've been sexually starving myself, disregarding my needs, because of opinions that don't matter.

"You're going to come for me, little witch." Gideon's voice is deep and demanding as he stimulates me higher and higher. My hips try to move. I'm stretched past any point I've felt before, but I need something more.

"I need—" Reason is merely a word with no relation to my world at all. My body is so on the edge, so needy and hungry.

"What do you need, Rose?"

We pant together.

"I need your cock, I need to be fucked—hard." The stretch is intense, but I need impact. I need the jarring sensation of being pummeled. I need the direct thrust of Gideon's cock to shatter me.

The words come out in a whimper and for the second time in a single night, the *sensations* change.

My wrists are released and I'm suddenly on my back with Gideon's bulk above me, conquering me just as fierce in the absence of his tentacles. His cock thrusts into me and the hardness hits me in the spot I need it. The sweet ache of the prior stretch mixes perfectly with the directness of this form.

"Yes!"

My mind dissolves into sensations of him and my body taking his. Gideon's movements are fast and intense. My nails scrape down his back and my body shatters with a scream. Gideon thrusts deep and holds himself inside, groaning as his cock kicks inside me. The heat of his release bathing my insides.

The world is blurry, and I blink, trying to catch my breath. Gideon's head falls in the crook of my neck, and the breath of the man I just met this morning rushes over the heated skin of my chest. He raises his head and makes a sound of concern, his hot hand stroking over my cheek.

"Rose?" He wipes away moisture, tears. "Are you okay?"

"Yes." The word comes out uneven but clear. "I just really needed that."

The truth of the statement echoes once I say it. The weight, the constant whirring of worry in my brain, has vanished and I float. The beautiful sensation won't last, but it's so precious that I can't help but be grateful for the fleeting lack of anxiety.

"Thank you."

Gideon laughs roughly. "I should be the one thanking you. Or maybe worshiping you."

I choke on a laugh and Gideon's thumb strokes over my cheek again.

I'm caught by him. He isn't teasing me. The fervent look on his face halts my laugh and he leans in. The touch of his lips to mine is soft. I open for him, needing this kiss, tasting my tears and this beautiful moment.

This beautiful moment that isn't really real.

I pull away and clear my throat. Gideon starts at the sound and lifts his body from mine. His cock slides wetly from me. I half expect the man to roll away and start the awkward after-sex ritual but Gideon starts touching me, massaging my wrists before moving to my arms.

As expertly as he seduced me, he unwinds and soothes my body.

"Well," I start. "I think that this agreement will work out between us really well."

My words sound teasing but echo hollow in my chest.

Gideon doesn't respond right away, just keeps touching me, massaging muscles in my hips. Easing the discomfort that I'd ignored while I straddled him.

"What if I say I want something more lasting than our agreement, Rose?"

Confusion, then hope, and finally utter panic seizes me. It's an incredibly nauseating mixture that drags me down from the high of sex and fantasy and back to reality.

If this isn't a fantasy, if this is real, I can fuck it up.

Gideon, the predator his creature is, takes in my stiffening and eases back.

"Never mind, little witch, it's a discussion for a different time. Don't worry about it right now."

His words soothe over me, like whispering to a frightened animal. They are frustratingly effective, but I'm also frustrated at my own reaction.

But… I might have another opportunity to not react as poorly.

A tiny light of hope makes itself at home in my chest. Maybe, just maybe, I can keep Gideon longer than I thought.

And maybe it will all go terribly wrong.

CHAPTER 11

GIDEON

Rose sleeps soundly, sprawled on top of me. I hold her in my arms. I have since her words started slurring and she rested her head on my chest with a small snore. I don't know if falling asleep together had been in her plans. If I wake her, will she pull away in the light of day?

I soak in the feel of her heartbeat and the tickle of her hair while I can.

Two steps forward, one step back. It's a precarious step too, one that brings me to the edge of a cliff. I saw it in her eyes when I suggested something more. Gaping terror. I won't know her reasons without asking, I can only sneak around in the dark.

Last night… had not gone how I had planned it. My methods are meticulous, rarely do I lose control of a situation, but my normally restrained self crumbles when faced with Rose. Getting jealous during sex, letting this woman egg me on until something ferocious wanted to do just what she had asked for. To fuck her like no one else had.

There is no regret stemming my blood, not a single one. The experience, seeing Rose's considering eyes take in my partially shifted form and shrug, is one that will live in a place of honor in my memory for the rest of my life. A wonder of a woman.

No regrets, but the time for strategy is upon me and I can't let myself mess it up.

There are no visible windows in this room, but daylight illuminates it all the same. Magic.

I watch as Rose's pale skin shows me more in the morning light. More freckles, more delicate curves. Her hair takes on the burning hue that first drew me toward her. A treasure.

One I cannot let get away.

I almost want to wake her just to see her smile. Brave and open even if she's been hurt before by this "perfect" mate. *Don't think about it, Gideon.*

Don't think about hunting the man down. Don't think about the possibility of him showing up again. If he shows up, will Rose go to him?

Stop.

Strategy and persistence. I'll woo my mate with strategy and persistence.

There will be no more losing control of the situation no matter how tempting the woman on top of me is. No matter how much my inner beast wants to steal her away and hoard her brightness.

Rose stirs as if privy to my urges. Her bleary eyes open and she takes in her surroundings, her brows furrowing in confusion.

"Did we both fall asleep?" Rose yawns and leans in when I massage her scalp.

"I was going to wake you soon." I skirt around the question.

Rose hums. "I need to go back to my place and change."

"I'll walk you."

Rose sits up, the curve of her breasts distracts me, and I almost miss her words.

"That's not necessary."

The more alert Rose becomes, the more I sense her pulling away.

"Uh, last night was really… nice." Rose's face flushes and she puts her hands to her cheeks, scowling. "Gods, that sounded bad. It was so much more than I expected."

I lift my brows at that, trying to keep my mouth from twitching.

Rose's brow scrunches. "Not that I expected something bad. That also sounds terrible. I need coffee—"

"I greatly enjoyed spending last night with you," I interrupt her and push a curl of her hair behind her ear. "And I'd greatly enjoy seeing you again. Can I bring you lunch?"

Rose widens her eyes in alarm.

"I can't do a repeat performance at lunch! I'm—" Her face turns even redder. "I'm too sore for that."

Concern immediately rises.

"Is it an uncomfortable amount of sore? Any sharp pains?"

Rose just blinks at me. "Uh, no. Just feeling a little stretched and raw."

There's a tiny bit of satisfaction that blooms in me at that, and I let myself chuckle.

"While I'd never say no to sexual intimacy with you, I was asking just about lunch as a mealtime not an afternoon delight."

"You want to bring me lunch?" Rose is surprised in a way that makes me want to grit my teeth.

She's too delightful of a woman to be so surprised by this. I need to get out of the category she's placed me in soon. The category that leaves no room for attachments.

"I want to see you again. Talk to you. We can go out instead if you'd rather."

"Either of those sound lovely."

CHAPTER 12

ℛOSE

I blink and then blink again. The computer screen stays the same, but my mind is now on my task instead of going on vacation while I scrolled through client information. For the moment anyway.

I'm supposed to be matching. Even with the amount of power we're going to get from Gideon's and my *activities,* I told Jared that I'd make more matches. But every single time I adjust in my comfy office chair, the twinges of my body remind me of last night.

We have some healing salves just for this purpose, but I want this small discomfort. I want the reminder. To remember the image of Gideon's body, the stretch of him inside me, the way he touched me, and called me a wonder.

Consequently, my ability to focus this morning is severely lacking.

Last night was everything I hoped for in a sexual encounter. So hot it knocked my socks off and with just enough comfort to keep me from being swamped with issues and past hurts. My insecurities left me for a precious amount of time, only to come rushing back when

Gideon asked about something more lasting than our agreement.

Frustration tastes bitter with a kick of spice. Frustration that I can't seem to be brave where I need to anymore. My lack of confidence is crumbling what I want in my life. My matching mojo, my ability to trust myself.

This is not sustainable. I'm not okay, I'm not managing, and I have to do something about it.

Next time Gideon brings up something "more lasting" I will not panic just because of the possibility of failure, of rejection.

If there is a next time.

Goddammit, Rose, you should just ask.

If this had all happened before the Jackson incident, I would have asked him what he meant. But now… the very concept of talking about something that leaves my desires so exposed constricts my throat. Because I *like* Gideon.

It shouldn't matter. We can't even bond. Or really, I don't want to ask if there is a way we can bond because then I'd have to admit that I want that.

I groan and rest my head on my desk. My mind is going in circles and this isn't helping at all with my need to make matches.

Deep breaths, Rose. Light a candle or something. Or I could brush my fingers over the paper I set out today. This stationery has an ocean theme with blue marbling and gold paper clips in the shapes of star fish. I itch to pick up the pen, but the gold brush pen I arranged this morning doesn't feel quite right.

Or I'm stalling.

A knock on my doorframe startles me and relief has me sighing. A distraction from the race of my thoughts is welcome.

Lowell's lips are pursed in annoyance and a woman fidgets behind him. She looks familiar and it takes me a moment to place her. The harpy from yesterday. What had been her name?

"We have an issue that I could use your help with." Lowell's voice bleeds annoyance as much as the look on his face. "You remember Sophia from yesterday? My wards caught her starting up a recording device in the main bath area, with Hall Newberry."

Groaning would be unprofessional, but now Lowell's mood makes sense. The hellish Newberrys.

"Can you deal with her while I deal with them?" Lowell asks.

Sophia's eyes widen with alarm when Lowell says, "deal with."

"Yes, have a seat, Sophia. Nonconsensual violence isn't allowed in the building, we have a ward against it, so try and relax," I say.

The sophisticated ward is custom made and priceless to this establishment. It keeps the bathhouse a safe place where someone can still get a consensual spanking. The ward master who did the work is truly talented. Even if his eyes widened at the request.

Sophia's shoulders relax slightly and Lowell snorts. "We're lovers, not fighters."

My lips tug up at that. Once upon a time, our ancestors used their magics to enact punishment in times of instability. They left behind that bloody history to start the bathhouse, to use their skills for something good. To be lovers instead of fighters.

Sophia drops into the chair across from me as Lowell leaves.

"Do you want to tell me why you brought a recording device into an area where it's expressly forbidden?" I ask, getting right to it.

The harpy starts to blush.

"Uh, for my own pleasure."

My blink is long. "Your ability to lie isn't great. Do you want to try and answer my question again?"

Her ability to lie is actually passable, but being able to see soul threads combined with looking for a deception means that she isn't hiding as much as she wants to from me.

Sophia compresses her mouth.

"Alright, I'm going to make some educated guesses then. I'm going to guess that you know Linda Newberry, that she is a friend…" I read Sophia's reaction. "Hm, client it is. That doesn't make this better. I'm going to guess she hired you to catch evidence of her husband cheating."

Sophia furrows her brows and starts to look alarmed.

I interpret that and continue, "Not cheating then. Maybe just a video of a suspect situation involving her husband. We take privacy very seriously."

If there were anyone in the baths that would care about being recorded, Lowell would have led with that. There are ways we deal with rule breakers. Usually, a warning is enough. The people who come here don't have very many places they can be their true selves and the most common rules broken are the small ones on accident. Such as, outing someone else's attendance to the bathhouse in gossip and similar things.

Those who break the biggest rules and do something illegal get reported to the Council. Jared has a working relationship with several Council officials who handle things.

Every rule in between is dealt with on a case-by-case basis. Some with bans, others with hexes that we don't admit to.

Breaking privacy is bad, but not the worst thing that's happened today. Lowell gets to deal with that part. I need the details to decide what kind of punishment fits Sophia's crime, because the harpy is a victim in this as well.

"The recording will be destroyed. But informed consent is something we consider sacred here and that factors into this situation."

I wait to see if Sophia wants to interject. The harpy looks a little ashamed but that's probably just because she was caught.

"I wasn't planning on recording anyone else."

I roll my eyes. "What a relief. So, Linda is your client?"

Sophia doesn't answer; I continue with my assumption.

"And Linda didn't mention that her husband and her like to play games involving competing with who can seduce a third party faster?"

"What?" Sophia sounds startled.

"I thought not. But just to be clear, you did not consent to being party to their game?" I ask.

Now the harpy is angry, her energies swirling all over the place. "No, I did not."

"Just as well. The couple will get their own punishment for disregarding the rules." I'm personally hoping for a lifetime ban and a particularly nasty hex since this isn't the couple's first offense.

"That does leave us with how to deal with your violation of our very clear, very understandable rules. Now—"

Sophia interrupts me. "I may be willing to trade information that would be valuable to this establishment."

I blink in surprise. "Oh?"

"It would be a mutually beneficial arrangement. I don't need anyone knowing that my clients were screwing with me, and you don't need anyone to know that I was able to smuggle a recording device into this place—"

"Watch your tone," I warn.

Sophia appears to backpedal. "Even though I was caught before I left. Perhaps we could agree not to involve the Council in this matter."

No laws have been broken, so the Council wouldn't have been involved anyway, but I nod. Curious.

"What kind of information?"

"There's some kind of issue with your magic currents here. My kind are sensitive to magic. There's a wall in the main bathhouse that I touched, it's pulling magic too hard. It sapped me pretty quickly and I didn't think that was how this operation worked."

Concern roars. This operation definitely doesn't work that way, that's dangerous.

"Show me."

***

I scowl at the tiled wall. Lowell runs his hands over it slowly, just like I had done. The variation of magic flow is small, but it's there. Note to self, harpies are *very* sensitive to magic.

Lowell's scowl matches mine.

"We're going to need to reset the wards on magic flow completely," Lowell mutters more to himself than anyone else.

"Can you patch it until tonight, or do we need to close the bathhouse now?"

"I can patch it until we complete the fix, but we'll need to have *him* come in." Lowell shakes his head.

I try not to smile and make a mental to-do list. We need to contact Jared because I'm pretty sure this drain is what is ruining our numbers. The *him* Lowell mentioned is our grumpy giant of a ward master. I don't even know the man's name; he just goes by his title.

I lift my brows; he's not going to like Lowell patching up his original work.

Lowell glares at me, following the thought.

"Uh, can I go now?" Sophia asks.

I almost forgot the harpy's presence.

"Not yet. We haven't talked about your punishment," I say.

"But—"

"Thank you for pointing out our issue, but like I said, we take privacy seriously here."

Sophia's eyes widen and she gestures to a noisy couple on the other side of the main bathing room. "I don't think they're bothered by a lack of privacy."

I try hard not to smile. I glance over to the spectacle of Wanda and her husband, Jason. I made their match a few years ago and they share a wicked streak for exhibitionism.

Jason makes eye contact and winks at me before devoting his attention to Wanda. He bends over her body, whispering in her ear, probably that they have an audience, and my friend moans. It's the little things that shorten my breath and cause a blush to rise to my cheeks. The determined way Jason's grip bites into his wife's hips as he thrusts home from behind as if he's claiming her. The absolute surrender of Wanda on her knees giving Jason what he wants.

It's so primal and forceful in nature. Like they're openly claiming each other. I wonder…

"Rose?" Sophia's voice snaps my attention back to her. She smirks at me and I laugh.

"Sorry, sometimes they're distracting."

"*I'm glad I'm not the only one,*" Sophia mutters. "So, what is your decree, oh strict witch?"

Right, back to business.

"What is your job, Sophia?"

"I get information, for a price. It's my business."

The proud way the harpy speaks, her boldness, and the mischievous air that is always present around her are all telling.

The woman isn't naïve, but there is an eagerness that is just begging to cause trouble. The kind of trouble the bathhouse does not need. Eagerness that needs to be tempered with something, some balancing force. A solution comes to mind.

"You're banned from this bathhouse until you're mated or settled with a long-term partner," I say.

"What! But you guys are all about inclusivity. It's on like, every flyer I have from here."

"Yes, but the nature of your work makes this complicated."

Sophia gapes at me before snapping her mouth shut. "You've effectively banned me for life."

"Not for life," I say.

"Harpies don't take mates or have long-term partners."

"Ah, well… that's unfortunate for the whole banning thing," I concede.

Sophia glares but something must occur to her because she tilts her head. "Never mind. This might work in my favor. I've got to start my reputation somehow."

I bark out a laugh. I'm almost a little sad that I'll probably never see this harpy again. I like her craftiness.

"Let me show you out then, oh banned patron."

I leave Lowell muttering obscenities at the wall.

CHAPTER 13

GIDEON

I stand in the lobby of the bathhouse with a bag of takeout, waiting for Rose. The woman with purple hair at the front desk said that she's busy. I check my watch again and worry starts to edge into my good mood. This is the time we arranged.

Did Rose regret last night? Is she trying to avoid me?

No. Rose won't avoid me. If she doesn't want to see me, she's allowed to call this whole agreement off. If she regretted anything, she'd do that.

My inner beast isn't helping with my logic. It just wants to wrap itself around Rose and never let go. Every moment we're separated while she doesn't know my true intentions itches with discomfort.

Rose enters the lobby with a familiar figure, and I fight to keep my expression neutral. *What is Sophia Shirazi doing here?*

"Gideon!" Rose's delight disperses some of my worries but not all.

Sophia shoots me a teasing look but has a poker face again when she speaks. "So, I can go now? Never to return again?"

Surprise breaks my own expression and Rose notices. I don't know what my face gives away exactly, but she narrows her eyes thoughtfully.

I used to be so good at covert operations. Either I'm terrible at them now or Rose is especially intuitive.

Rose waves a hand at Sophia. "For what it's worth, I do hope you can come back sometime."

The scoff Sophia gives echoes off the lobby walls. "Not likely."

The harpy proudly walks out the doors and a woman in a sharp business suit and enough sexual energy to power a small revolution walks in. Katherine, Rose's friend from the coffee shop.

"Oh, give me a second," Rose says to me.

"Rose, it's so good to see you." The dark-haired woman swoops Rose into her arms and they hug.

"It's good to see you too. This isn't the usual time you come in, I don't think there are any available people to partner with. Though if you're in a mood to watch, Jason and Wanda are at it."

The woman laughs throatily before casting her eyes to me in an appraising way. "No one available?"

Rose's smile turns brittle at the edges. "No one. This is Gideon. He and I are…" Rose trails off, not seeming to know how to identify our relationship.

"We're seeing each other," I finish, trying to keep my frustration from showing. I switch the takeout bag to my other hand and offer a handshake to the woman.

"I'm Katherine, I've known Rose for years." Katherine takes my hand, transitioning seamlessly from seductress to beaming friend. She turns to Rose and lifts her brows in a teasing look before continuing. "I'm actually here for business. Jared hired me."

"Oh, he did?"

Katherine casts me a look. "He called the firm
yesterday to help with the numbers he's looking into."

The vague statement piques my interest, but I don't
have a right to know anything about the bathhouse
business.

"Oh!" Rose exclaims. "I thought you said your firm was
busy lately. I'm surprised he could get you at such short
notice."

Katherine's shoulders drop. "Everyone with applicable
skills has been contracted out for a missing person. I'd
love to help them, but numbers and management are my
expertise."

"Another missing person? That's terrible!" Rose says.

I narrow my eyes and make a note to myself to check
if there are many paranormals going missing lately. Most
families hire third parties to find missing members if
they feel the Council isn't making the effort they want. A
missing person in the same city as Rose doesn't bode well
for my instincts. They could have run away... or something
else could be going on.

"Yes, it is. My teammates did say they feel like they're
making some headway, though." Katherine offers a sad
smile.

There's a pause in the conversation. The topic of
missing people in the paranormal community is one that
causes a shiver to race down the backs of even those born
after the time the Council was created.

Rose shakes her head before continuing.

"Well, we may have found the drain. We won't be sure
until Lowell can really take apart our wards though," Rose
addresses me. "Our numbers for magic gathered have been
off. Jared, he's the man who sent you back to my office

yesterday, is running an investigation. Hopefully we can get this patched up soon."

Warmth rises in my chest and chases away some of the cold worry. Rose trusts me, trusts me enough to impart this detail about her business.

Katherine makes a sound of disappointment. "That's a pity. I mean, it's great that you think you've found the issue, but I was looking forward to long work nights with your brother. You really should have introduced me to him earlier, Rose."

Rose laughs. "Jared doesn't participate in bathhouse antics, ever. Lowell's in the main bathhouse investigating if you need to talk to him though."

Katherine shrugs. "I'll proceed with business like usual. If it turns out this isn't what's causing the error, I can still put together my own report and turn it into your brother."

The woman bids us a farewell and Rose and I head back to her office.

"You wouldn't rather eat in a break room?"

"I like the privacy of my office and I need to call Jared about the drain, if you don't mind. I'm sorry, things have been hectic today."

I enjoy Rose's office; it smells of her. Rose sighs. "It's a pity I'm not allowed to match Jared. He and Katherine would be so good together."

"You might not need to. Katherine doesn't appear to be a woman who will let someone she wants get away from her."

Rose snickers. "Truer words have never been spoken."

I set up the food on Rose's giant desk while she makes the phone call. Her brother is curt on the other end but there is a sense of relief to their conversation. The stationery on the other side of Rose's desk has me smiling.

I noticed her extensive collection of paper products the last time I was here. It brought to mind a perfect courting gift. A gift that is now burning a hole in my pocket.

I drag a chair around the desk so we can sit on the same side.

My first instinct is to demand Rose sit on my lap but I'm trying to express my interest past the physical. Rose and I are incredibly compatible when it comes to sex, more so than I ever dreamed. But I need her to realize we can have more than that.

Rose falls down into her chair with a sigh. "I'm so relieved that that's dealt with. Or at least, that we're starting to deal with it."

I pass her a carton and she inhales the scent of the food appreciatively. Making a sound of pleasure that has my body priming itself. *Focus, Gideon.*

"This is from my favorite restaurant!" Rose takes a bite and makes another suggestive sound that has me readjusting in my seat. "It's like you've been watching me or something."

Her words take me by surprise, and I try not to react. I've been deemed a mysterious bastard more than once, but that persona evaporates when it comes to Rose. She arches an eyebrow while she chews her bite of food. When she swallows, she sets aside the carton.

"Would you like to confess something, Gideon? Maybe how you know that hellion Sophia Shirazi?"

A flush spreads up my neck. Rose is connecting the dots aptly, with accuracy.

Confess. If she runs, steal her. Half of that inner thought is a good idea.

I should confess to following—stalking—her. But… the way she pulled away last night comes to mind.

"I know Sophia. I've hired her for information before in... treasure hunting."

Rose nods. "I thought you might know her. She seems like a handful and a half."

My face cracks into a grin. "I also received that impression."

I swallow. I want to confess to watching Rose, but I can't risk her reaction. Yet.

Rose makes a thoughtful sound and continues eating. I take a bite of the food but can't eat more. My insides twist at deceiving my mate.

After a nauseating amount of time, Rose sets down her chopsticks.

"Why me?" Rose asks and the topic skirts my own thoughts about confessing so closely that I almost drop the chopsticks.

The question hovers between us.

"I'm sorry if it seems like I'm asking out of nowhere, but my mind keeps coming back to it. Is it just... convenience?" Rose winces.

A growl rumbles through my chest before I suppress it. My primal nature slips at the ache in her question.

"No. It's not convenience."

She'd asked me this yesterday. My original answer had been clumsy. *Why not you?* Had been a terrible attempt in cloaking my intentions through misdirection. But I had told her that my instincts wanted her. A correct sentiment that only touches the surface of my intention.

I need to dig deeper, expose more, give Rose the heart I'm trying to clumsily offer her. I open my mouth to do just that and snap it shut. Rose tilts her head in question.

Last night I tried to ask Rose about being in a relationship and she panicked before I even got close to

the important statements. What's to stop her from doing
the same thing? If I say I want to claim her as my mate,
will she shut me out?

"Can I answer that later?" My voice sounds rough, my
throat tight with indecision.

Rose's brows lift high at that.

"I'll answer your question, I promise, I'm just…"

*Hesitant to have this woman flee from me? To widen an
unbridgeable schism if I come on too strong?*

"Approaching with caution?" Rose suggests.

I sigh in relief. "Yes. Exactly that."

Rose looks at me speculatively and I have the sense
that she's interpreting exactly what my fears are in relation
to her. It's eerie but welcome since she doesn't look as
if she'll run from me. It feels as if we've reached an
understanding without me saying the words that would
scare away my mate.

Rose shrugs. "We have time. Two more nights
according to the agreement."

I don't allow myself to grimace at that. I have no
intention of letting Rose go once the agreement is fulfilled.

Rose breaks into that determined thought. "But we
can't meet tonight. I'll be busy helping with the wards."

I nod easily. "I have some things I need to do for work
as well." Illegal things. "Though I'd much rather be with
you."

Rose's eyes sparkle. "I bet. Can you tell me anything
about your current job?"

I shrug. My work doesn't require confidentiality.

"I'm tracking down an amulet that a client of a client
had stolen. There's going to be an auction in another
couple of weeks at the antique shop next door."

Rose frowns. "Should we be worried? That something illegal is happening next door?"

I shake my head. "From what I know, the auction is perfectly legal. The artifacts probably have a false provenance. Nothing to be alarmed about yet."

We continue our lunch and trading questions. I learn about the history of the bathhouse; how it's been passed down the last few generations of the Love family. I tell her about the seaside cottage that is technically my home that I spend almost no time in.

"Do you always live on the coast?" she asks.

"More often than not, but it's not a requirement. I don't have a siren call to the ocean. It's just comforting." I'll stay in this rainy city and live with Rose since this is her family's business. Not that she's asked me to stay here once my business is done.

Rose hums at my answer and I distract her with the tale of finding a witch's family spell book that had been stolen. That mission had ended well, but had the inconvenience of me being cursed with truth-telling that had taken an hour for my power to dispel.

Rose's laughter at my inadvertently insulting that witch's grandmother's stew was well worth the humiliating tale.

When I've put away the last of the empty cartons and Rose's desk is again spotless, I make my move. I slide my hand in my hanging coat pocket and bring out the rectangular case.

"I have something for you," I say.

Rose frowns. "Gideon."

I freeze, the wooden box in my hands now feels heavy. Will she not accept my offering?

Rose looks at my gift, conflicted. "I-I don't do the things we did in exchange for *things*, for payment."

Anger cracks through me. "You think I'm trying to pay you?"

Confusion blooms on my Rose's face.

"You're not?" Rose shakes her head. "I just—I want it clear that I didn't agree to anything for payment or even in exchange for the magic. I have nothing against sex work as a concept, but I don't want that in my intimacy. I called you because I wanted to."

The anger is still there, crackling under the surface of my skin, sparking and wanting to ignite even as I take a breath. Part of the anger is offense, and part is frustration. If I could have approached Rose, if I thought she had been open to a relationship, I would have.

Instead, I had to scheme and strategize to the point that my mate thinks my gift is the equivalent to tipping her for a job well done.

I push down the feelings and try to embrace that Rose just confessed to wanting me. To wanting the arrangement just to experience what we could have together.

The creature is still irritated.

I take another breath and blow it out. "This isn't a payment."

Rose's cheeks pinken. "I'm starting to understand that. I didn't mean to offend you—"

"It's a gift."

"Gideon! That's still payment."

"It's a courting gift!" The words come out loud and hoarse. I bite my tongue.

Rose falls silent, eyes wide.

She blinks. "A what?"

I open the case to keep my mouth from giving any more of my intentions away.

Rose gasps.

Revealed on velvet are two fountain pens. I custom ordered the pieces in the early nineteen-hundreds, made with pink marble and gold. One is a serviceable, thinner pen, kept plain except for some gold decorating the naturally occurring veins. The other is the showpiece, with small octopus shapes inlaid with white and gold that spiral around the body of the pen. Each shape set with an emerald eye. The cap and the end have engraved gold octopuses.

The artistry of the piece is profound, each detail, every tiny tentacle, delicately wrought.

Rose reaches for the gift with shaking hands and stops, glancing up at me as if asking permission. Her eyes are wet and face full of awe.

I push it forward into her hands, not trusting myself to say anything else and break the moment.

Rose grips the case and swallows. "They're so beautiful." She runs a finger along the intricate design. "So perfect."

The anger and irritation of a moment ago leave me. My creature is practically purring in pleasure.

Rose starts to shake her head. "But they're too nice—"

A sharp primal sound escapes me and Rose jumps. The look I must give her must quiet any arguments because she only bites her lip.

"Do I have permission to give you gifts?" I force levity into my voice.

Rose's eyes are owlishly wide, and she looks down at the pens again.

"Well, if I say yes now, it makes me appear greedy."

I cup Rose's face and she pulls her gaze away from the shiny pens.

"Nothing wrong with a little greed, Rose." I let the words roll off my tongue and the flush that rises in her face fills me with satisfaction. "You deserve to be wooed and I mean to woo you."

It's as much as I dare to say about my intentions, but Rose looks as if she understands. A calm settles over me.

Good.

***

I case out the antique store from the coffee shop, muttering to myself about courting gifts and strategy. I wait until the human worker locks the place up and leaves. I'd rather have passed the time watching Rose and her cousin reset the wards to fix the magic drain, but we're not quite at that place in our relationship yet. The place where my watching Rose do mundane things for hours would be sweet instead of alarming.

The magic drain they're dealing with is an odd business and I wouldn't want to distract them anyway. Rose told me that the drain could have been created organically, a misplaced symbol or wards mixing badly, or purposefully.

In my experience, large amounts of something valuable going missing is the result of thievery, not accident. But I am most often involved in issues of tracking down objects that are stolen, not objects that have been misplaced; no matter how much Rose teases about finding her keys.

I walk across the street casually and down the alley between the bathhouse and the antique store. The side door of the store isn't in the public view. It's still warded and locked, but at least I don't need to worry about being seen by any passerby intuitive enough to see through my shielding.

The ward on the building is a good one, but nothing like masterful ones on the bathhouse.

My being reaches through the strands of magic that make up the ward. I hadn't lied when I told Rose that my kind are more magic than not. A trait we share with cephalopods is our ability to get into anywhere we wish. The door unlocks, and I slide effortlessly through the wards in a matter of moments.

The darkness in the store doesn't bother me. My night vision is good enough to avoid crashing into anything. I get to the office with no issues, and I flick the light switch. There are no windows in this room and the light will make it easier to use my phone camera if I find what I'm looking for.

I don't trust the information we were given by the informant. With this place being right next to my mate, I let my suspicions run rampant.

The office contrasts with Rose's cozy one. There is a warped desk stacked with messy folders of random, useless information. Discarded timecards and receipts from shipping companies aligning with the month this place opened. The carpet underfoot is the generic tight kind that has begun to fray with age. Nothing in this building appears to have been updated with the opening of the store.

The air is stale in here. This isn't an office someone works in regularly, rather, it's a part of the façade that this store is. And if they need a whole store to disguise this auction… this location might be edging more toward illegal activity than I anticipated.

The lack of a computer is another marker toward the seediness of the business. Paper records are king.

I continue searching. The safe is easy to crack but doesn't yield what I want. On a whim, I look in the office vents and roll my eyes. Sure enough, I pull out a stack of papers after unscrewing the cover.

Magic and all other options available, and they choose to hide things in air vents.

All the files for the auction are here. The owners of the store are the same people acting as auction hosts. A Mark and Jackson Dewitt are the listed names, though they could be aliases. I take photos of the official papers before leafing through the item list for the auction.

There is a section at the end that makes me frown. It's using some sort of code that looks vaguely familiar in place of an item description, so I take a photo of that as well.

After getting the photos, I'm about to slide the folders back in their hiding place when the date listed for the auction catches my eye. I spit out a curse.

I wrap up everything quickly and am soon walking down the street back to Mace's empty townhouse. He picks up my call and I start in without greeting him.

"The auction has been moved up. It's in two days."

Mace curses on the other end.

"I'm sending you some photos of the auction list and other official documents now. The section at the bottom is giving me a bad feeling."

There is a pause, Mace looking over the information, before a heavy sigh.

"Well, this is much worse than I thought it'd be."

CHAPTER 14

ROSE

Happiness hums through me as surely as my yawn. My eyes are scratchy, and my body begs me for a nap, but satisfaction warms me. I balance two mugs of tea and make my way to the lobby.

Lowell looks up from the front desk, looking just as tired as I feel.

"Please tell me this is one of Jared's high caffeine blends?" His voice is rough from lack of sleep and arguing with the ward master. Who, predictably, did not appreciate Lowell patching the ward yesterday.

At my nod, Lowell accepts the mug with a grateful groan. We've been here with the ward master since we closed late last night. Trading off duties for naps.

The payoff is worth the sleep. We're able to open this morning with full confidence that our issue is fixed. The ward master is doing one last check over and Lowell is sending out notifications that we're now open.

The ward master added an overlaying ward to keep such an event from occurring again. He says the siphoning was purposefully set up and had to have been done from the inside of the bathhouse. Jared is furious. He's locked himself in the business office and is calling contacts to track down who or what group would dare do such a thing. I don't think he's slept yet.

I foresee many tea blends coming from this. Jared uses the hobby to calm himself down and set aside stress. I take a satisfying sip of this particular blend and hum. It's an invigorating floral mixed black tea with a citrus kick.

"You're sure happy on this cloudy morning." Lowell's eyes narrow. His bad mood is from clashing with the ward master.

The ward master's methods are meticulous to my cousin's free-form process. There has been a lot of snapping and snarking between the two of them all night. Even with the men trying my patience, I'm floating on a cloud.

I stare into my swirling tea. Happy. "Things are just resolving themselves nicely."

"How so?" he asks.

"Well, we've solved the drain issue, so I'm not under so much pressure to make matches."

Lowell waits for more. There is more but that really could be enough.

"I'm revising my matching strategy. Looking more into what the people wanting to be matched say they want versus what they need in their life, instead of relying so much on compatibility readings." I've done that before, but this time I'm putting more emphasis on it.

I've been focusing so much on my lack of confidence in compatibility reading, letting doubts freeze me, that I let it overshadow every tool I use to match. Current events have shaken me out of my matching rut.

"Well, that should help your overflowing inbox. And…?" Lowell says, eyes sparkling with glee. His bad mood beginning to fade.

I duck my head but smile. "I think Gideon really likes me."

"Oh really?"

"You know, past the number of nights we agreed on. Like, a relationship." My cheeks heat.

Lowell's brows lift, unsurprised, but it had felt more like a revelation to me. Gideon *likes* me, likes me, and not even hearing that someone has been stealing from us is enough to dim my mood.

I might not know why Gideon approached me in particular, but his reluctance to answer the question when I had panicked the last time he brought up anything more permanent has a warmth kindling in my chest.

Because I *like* like Gideon. It's quick, but everything he shows me about himself draws me in. It's not because of the pens he gave me, though the addition to my collection is so perfect and thoughtful that I almost cried.

It's the *care* Gideon gives me. How conscientious he is about my well-being, the way he can bring a smile to my face with words. If I were looking to match myself, with no thought to soul thread compatibility, Gideon would be who I'd want.

I've always been decisive about my emotions. My lack of decisiveness these last few months has contributed to my unhappiness, a spiral of doubt.

It makes me want to take risks. I hear a shuffle just inside the public bathing room and make my decision quickly.

"So, Lowell, you told me you wanted to be matched."

The other room drops into silence and my cousin snorts in his tea and coughs.

After clearing his throat, Lowell shakes his head. "Oh, so now that you've figured your stuff out, you feel like meddling again?"

It's an accurate statement but I just lift my brows at him until he starts to fidget.

Lowell sighs. "Yes, I'm open to it."

We'll see about that.

"There's a match I've always thought would work out really well."

Lowell stills, hope clear on his face. "Really?"

I look into my tea. I want my cousin to be happy and this could be a fantastic match. I push onward.

"You know I don't usually match those who haven't expressed an interest, but… what do you think of our ward master?"

I wince at Lowell's laugh, but he cuts himself off.

"Oh, you're serious! Rose, he hates me!"

I hum, thinking of the secret glances the both of them give each other when the other isn't looking.

"I don't think he does," I say. "So, you're not interested in him?"

Lowell scowls at me. "Of course I'm interested in him! I've been interested in him since the start. He's gorgeous and a genius even if he's the biggest grouch I've ever met."

Gorgeous? Really? I mean, maybe I could see it. The ward master is big and rugged, but I've never spent much time looking at him. There's a glamour on him of some kind that is probably a combination that disguises what type of paranormal he is and makes people avert their eyes. Can Lowell see through it?

"But that doesn't change the fact that he hates me. Unless you've already forgotten, he and I have just spent all night griping at each other—" Lowell cuts off and blushes when the man in question enters the room.

The ward master strolls toward Lowell's spread leg position on the stool, stepping into his space. He takes my cousin's mug of tea from his hands and brings it up to his own mouth.

Lowell's blush deepens when the ward master presses his mouth to where his had just been and drinks from it before licking the rim of the mug and setting it on the front desk. The sexual tension has my own skin flushing. Should I look away?

"Your wards are done. Don't fuck with them." And with that, the man leaves out the front door.

Lowell and I stare at each other, wide eyed, before he glares at me.

"Oh you—I can't believe you just set me up like that." Lowell breaks his glare to stare at the front door, a thoughtful look on his face.

"And…" I trail off.

Lowell scrunches his brow. "I can't decide if I should fuck with the wards to have him come in again, or just call him."

Relief has me smiling. "Maybe start with figuring out what his name is."

Lowell makes a sound of agreement.

This is who I am, matching likely couples and letting them figure it out.

I'm finally starting to feel like myself again. Like I'm on solid footing.

That footing cracks when a man walks into the lobby. Lowell swears under his breath as Jackson strides to the front desk. The Jackson that took all my openness, my hopes, and body, and threw it out like day-old trash.

The Jackson I assumed I'd never see again.

He's still handsome but I can't help but compare him to Gideon. Jackson's looks are superficial compared to the thrum of Gideon's intensity, an intensity that rattles me to my core. Looking at the man who broke my heart, now all I can see is how shallow his presence is.

This is the man whose voice I hear in my head? That's given me so many issues? Who influenced my abstinence until Gideon showed up? I'm vaguely disappointed in myself.

I let myself really see Jackson when he stops at the desk. Under the thin, attractive veneer, the man looks like shit. There are dark circles under his eyes and his skin has taken on a sickly color.

"Ah, Rose, it's good to see you." Jackson's smile is stiff and fake.

"Uh…" *Good to see me?* Anger bubbles up and ties my tongue at the greeting.

"I'm just checking in to see how you are. I have a client coming in tonight and was wondering if I could get a tour of the bathhouse and make sure it would fit his needs."

"You want a tour?" I ask in disbelief. Jackson told me that this place was no better than a brothel. Right before he told me I wasn't the kind of woman he'd marry.

Jackson clears his throat, and I have an urge to punch him. I breathe out, willing myself to let the violence go. I wouldn't let this man, or anyone he brings, patron this bathhouse even if we didn't have a history.

"That isn't a good idea." My voice is stern and clear. "You'll need to find another establishment to bring your clients. This one runs on mutual respect."

An ugly look crosses Jackson's face before it disappears just as quickly.

"Oh Rose, don't be dramatic. I regret how things ended between us."

He regrets that things ended? Or that he ripped apart my heart?

Anger at myself stirs. I've been wallowing for months over this man. I shouldn't have let this man's judgment hurt me. I should have used all my senses instead of just reading our compatibility. I'm partially responsible for my own heartbreak and I accept that.

Jackson's presence now is like nails on a chalkboard.

And he's still talking.

"And I was hoping I could take you out, on a date." He dangles the offer in front of me with a knowing smirk.

A date in public. We didn't go on any dates before. When I asked to, he told me he didn't want anyone to see us together. I asked why not but he had only laughed.

I should have broken it off then. Instead, I let my imagination run wild. Telling myself some story about how we were seeing each other in secret for now, until it was a good moment for me to meet Jackson's family. I was so determined to believe in Jackson's good intentions that I ignored every single slight.

Fuck this guy.

Jackson looks expectant, smiling. I don't know how I didn't see this man's sliminess. I smothered my own good sense at the idea of a perfect match.

"I'm not interested in going out with you."

Lowell lets out a relieved sigh.

Jackson's face morphs in surprise until it stretches in scowling disgust.

It's in the face of his disgust that I notice a striking detail. His soul threads are a sickly yellow and stiff, completely different than they were when I met him. Completely incompatible with my own soft pink threads that reach out so optimistically into the world.

I blink in confusion. Soul threads can change over time, but I've never seen such a large change in the span of a few months. The tempo of his threads no longer beat in time to mine at all.

A fluke. My perfect match was just a mistake.

My relief is absolute and reverberates through me.

Jackson opens his mouth, probably to spill his particular brand of degrading malice when the front door swings open.

Jared storms into the lobby, a thunderous expression on his face.

"What the fuck are you doing here?" My normally logical, if high strung, brother shouts.

The heat from my anger abates in the face of my brother's. Jackson starts stammering, but my brother isn't having it.

"Get out of our establishment and never come back!"

Something about the force that Jared says that must startle Jackson because he stumbles back.

"Y-you can't tell me what to do."

Jared gets right up in Jackson's face. "Oh, I can't, can I? You come around here again and I'm going to dig through your life so completely and recklessly until I find whatever shit you're trying to hide with your slimy smiles and shake it all loose. I'll expose every wrong thing you've ever done until you're ruined. And if I don't find anything, I'll make something up. Leave. Now."

"F-fine. I'm leaving." Jackson's posture is like a dog with its tail between its legs as he leaves.

The lobby falls quiet except for Jared's huffing. Did he run to get here?

"You'll make something up, huh?" I ask, my mouth curving.

Jared snorts. "I wouldn't have to."

I stare at my brother. He'd never just make something up. Jared Love is one of the most moral people I know.

"I didn't need you doing that. But I really appreciate it," I say.

Jared's face turns pink and I round the desk to give him a hug.

"Thank you."

"Anytime," Jared mutters.

"Is that the only reason you came over here?"

My brother's face goes from pink to red. "Uh, yes. Lowell texted me."

Lowell smiles. "Had to call in a fighter instead of a lover. Though…" A mischievous look crosses his face. "Maybe we should have called in your lover instead."

How would Gideon react? Would he storm in here in a jealous rage? Or maybe he'd flex that power that rests just below the surface and Jackson would mysteriously disappear.

"You're seeing someone?" Jared asks.

Now I'm the one blushing.

"It's still new," I say.

"I'm happy to hear that." Jared's shoulders drop in relief. "Really happy."

I poke him, still high on my success with Lowell. "Happy enough to let me match you?"

Jared huffs but looks away. It's such a different reaction than his angry refusals before that I can only blink.

"Wait, are you seeing someone too?"

Jared makes a face. "I… it's up in the air. I'll tell you when things land."

Curiosity takes bites from my restraint, but the conflicted look in Jared's eyes eases my sisterly nosiness. Next time he won't be so lucky, but for now I can wait until he figures out his shit.

Lowell has none of my current restraint though. He grins. "If it's Katherine, don't bother trying to escape from her. That woman knows what she wants and isn't afraid to use every trick in the book."

Jared's ears turn red and he curses before turning. "I'm going back to the office. Call me if you need me."

When he's gone, I take in Lowell's expression.

I can't keep from checking. "So, no jealousy about Katherine?"

"Oh, I have a ward master to figure out." Lowell's brows descend in thought before raising with cheer. "And just think how much she's going to ruin Jared's orderly life."

I bite my lips. "It might not be her."

We share a look and dissolve into quiet laughter. If anyone could put that conflicted look on Jared's face since the last time I saw him, it's Katherine.

They'll be a wonderful match as long as Jared can get out of his own way.

Am I in my own way? The answer is so clear now.

I didn't fuck up my chance at love. Jackson was never my soul mate. It was all just a mistake. A misreading.

I take a deep breath and sigh it out. The breath leaves my lips and takes with it a tangle of emotions that have weighed me down for so long I thought that the heavy feeling was normal. So much fear and shame for so little reason.

Without the weight on my chest, the fear dogging my steps, clarity rises.

I won't waste any more time or emotional energy on the likes of Jackson. That part of my life is done with.

And if I'm not constantly in a state of fear that I'll fuck up a good thing… I know exactly what I want. I don't know if a mating is really possible, but I won't waste time dithering about it.

I tap out a text and make myself send it before taking a calming breath and sipping my hot tea.

Be brave, Rose.

CHAPTER 15

GIDEON

The patience I pride myself in has deserted me.

The tapping of my fingers on the countertop starts to gain watchers, so I squeeze my hand in a fist and try to control myself. I sit in my usual stool at the coffee shop, keeping a passive watch of the antique store. That this location lets me watch the bathhouse is an added benefit I savor.

My beast wants nothing more than to go across the street to hunt my mate, but I have responsibilities. Responsibilities that weigh far heavier than they did when it was only artifacts being sold at the auction.

Mace confirmed the bad feelings I had about the encoded items on the list. The auction is trafficking people.

I grit my teeth. The underbelly of the paranormal world is something I'm far too familiar with. Every time I turn around there is some group selling another as objects. You'd think that after thousands of years, the practice would die already. But every time the authorities or *others* stomp out a seller, another takes their place.

We planned on attending the auction and just bidding to buy back the artifacts but that isn't going to happen now that this auction is also selling *people*.

Now there will be conflict, and my inner beast is ready to tear them apart if needed.

It probably won't be needed.

We have a plan. It's nothing we haven't dealt with before.

It's better not to ponder that this is all happening right next door to my mate.

The reason for my impatient tapping.

I want to see her, to hold her, to reassure myself that she's unharmed. My logical side knows that she's just fine, that we've been texting back and forth about getting together for tonight.

Tonight, when Mace said he'll take over the watch. Though my responsibilities are now greater, I will not give up any time in wooing my mate. Not when I seem to be gaining ground. The first text of today sings through me.

Are you available tonight? I miss you.

I miss you. I shouldn't be as hopeful about that one line, but it's the first inclination that Rose wants me for more than sex.

A man walks in front of the antique store for the second time within the last few minutes. My instincts prick. It's possibly nothing, but when he ducks into the alley between the antique store and the bathhouse, I'm already moving.

I get to the alley in the blink of an eye and take a photo of the man. Usually, that would be enough. Mace would identify a suspect and our covert operation would still be intact. But this man frowns at the brick siding of the bathhouse and a surge of protectiveness has me moving to engage.

"What are you doing?" I try to not let aggression bleed into my voice. Based on the way the man jumps, I've failed.

"I-I'm just on a walk. Not that it's any of your business."

"On a walk down an alleyway? How scenic."

The man sneers at me. "Do you even know who I am?"

I lift my eyebrows. "Someone acting suspicious."

"I'm Jackson Dewitt."

Dewitt, Dewitt, Dewitt. An old family that has some nominal standing in the paranormal and human community. I honestly only know that much because of Mace's research on the owners of the antique store. Jackson and Mark Dewitt, our targets for the auction. And he's currently sneaking around Rose's bathhouse.

A man involved with slavery is near Rose.

Calm, Gideon. Remember the plan.

"I own this city," Jackson spits.

That's an exaggeration. But as much as I want to, I can't kill this man where he stands just to keep him away from Rose. There are such things as laws in this modern world and we need him to bring the captives to this location or we'll lose our chance to free them.

A small encouragement to keep him away from Rose though... that I can do. My magic swells and the air takes on the flavor of a compulsion.

"Jackson Dewitt, you will stay away from this bathhouse."

The expression on Jackson's face transitions from confused disgust into a dazed neutral look before fear takes over. It's difficult to be the creature that I am and perform coercive magic without some bit of fear tucked in. In this instance, I don't regret the effect.

Dewitt stumbles backward, and I let him flee. He probably won't even remember why he's running. My compulsions can be unpredictable, like the rest of my magic, but I'm sure enough that Jackson Dewitt is going to stay away from Rose that I relax.

It disturbs me that this Dewitt character seemed to be scoping out the bathhouse. Could the auction and the drain have the same culprits responsible? I draft a quick email to Mace and send the photos of the man before sending a message to Rose's business email with the details of the auction and the suspect.

I hesitate before pressing send but complete the action. I was going to share the details when I saw Rose next. It would have been an opportunity to confess about past activities that Mace and I have been involved in.

Dangerous activities that Rose deserves to know about. But safety supersedes convenience. It's better if she's aware of the threat now.

I head back to my position at the coffee shop to keep watch until Mace can relieve me.

Rereading Rose's texts won't help my impatience, but I can't help myself when it comes to my witch. My phone lights up with a new message. I frown, it's too soon for Rose to have read the email.

Rose: I have something I want to try tonight during our... session.

My cock hardens at the tease and I roll my eyes at myself before typing out a response.

What?

Rose: I'll tell you when we go back to the bathhouse.

I blow out a breath in frustration but smile. The waiting for tonight might be a cruel tease with my mind wondering what Rose could possibly ask to do, but my witch is going to ask for something. That she trusts me enough to do that is a step that I won't take lightly.

CHAPTER 16

ROSE

Fuck, fuck, fuck.

Gideon is going to show up at the bathhouse any minute and I'm a mess.

The plan is to go to the Thai place down the street for dinner. It'll be a nice date. Talking. We're going to talk and get to know each other better. I can ask questions about his life and tell him about some of the better matches I've made and, and, and…

I'm so horny. Distractingly, achingly, horrifyingly *horny*.

Our texts back and forth all day have been tame, but the effortless conversation style too easily brings back memories of the night we spent together. Too easily reminds me of the way he licked me so hungrily after coaxing me past my nerves. Too easily makes me think of what I want to suggest for tonight, even if I'm leery to.

I don't know if Gideon will think it's as hot as I do. He might not be comfortable with it, but Gideon deserves to be the one to say yes or no. I have to trust in his ability to make the decision that is right for him.

And to trust that he does want me to make requests.

Until we return to the bathhouse, I need to think about non-arousing thoughts. Not think about the way my skin is hot or that I ache between my legs when I remember the sight of Gideon stretching me, his tentacles. I shiver.

The knock at my office signals my doom. Gideon stands there looking good enough to eat. I admired his form the first day he came into my office but now that I've seen how he looks out of his clothes, he's temptation personified.

Date first. Then sexual entanglements.

"Gideon." I stand and walk over, wanting to throw myself at him. Should I tempt fate and kiss him? Probably not, but I lean in anyway.

Gideon grabs my arms and stops the kiss. He inhales and his eyes dilate.

"Rose."

My name comes out like a growl.

Oh, no.

"You can smell…" I mean to ask, but my face is on fire and embarrassment claws up my throat

Gideon laughs without humor. "Smell you? I can practically taste you on the air."

Of course he has super senses. Of course he can smell that I'm wet and so on the edge with arousal that I'm having a hard time thinking straight.

I squirm and his hands tighten on my arms in a way that has my imagination running away from me.

"I can't help it," I say, my voice small but breathy.

Gideon backs me up slowly until I'm against the front of my desk. The air is thick and my body aches for more contact. He leans his face closer to mine before burying it in the crook of my neck and inhaling. My knees go weak.

"So needy," Gideon says before giving a sharp nip to my earlobe that makes me gasp. "Deliciously needy. Maybe I should give you a small taste of what you're lusting after, something to take the edge off before dinner. What do you say, little witch? Do you want my mouth on you?"

His body presses against mine, setting off fireworks of hot sensations.

"Yes," I whisper before my mind brings up the situation of leaving for dinner after giving into the pull between us.

"I mean, no." I push back at him a little. Gideon doesn't budge but he releases his grip on my arms. I lean back on the desk and bring my legs up around his hips, pulling him by his coat to press against me. "How about we get a private room now?"

I run my fingers up his neck and through his hair. Gideon's eyes half-lidded with pleasure and his body rocks into the cradle of my thighs before he stills.

"No date?"

I whimper. "We can have a date another time. I need—fuck, I need you."

Gideon's mouth twists wryly. "I'm more than a walking cock, Rose."

My face must be as red as a tomato with how it burns. The shame that slithers up my spine isn't a bad sensation but a tickling tease in my belly that has my arousal surging.

"Please, Gideon," I beg.

Gideon's smile falls, in its place is an intense look that has me clenching on emptiness. He runs his hands up my legs before squeezing my hips. The grip has me moaning.

"How can I say no when you beg so prettily? Some questions first." Gideon takes a breath, as if he's trying to focus. "Are you hungry? I won't have my m—I won't disregard your other needs."

Excitement blurs my curiosity for whatever he was going to say, and I tug on his silky hair playfully. "I'm hungry for something other than food right now. We can order pizza if we need to."

"And what did you want to try tonight, little witch?"

My mind stumbles at that question and nerves start to bubble up in me, mixing with the desire.

"Uh—"

Gideon's laughter echoes through my body, deep and voracious. "Now you're shy?"

I tuck my heated face into his chest before trying to speak again. "Can we get to the room first?"

Gideon's laugh softens as he cradles me into his chest.

"Anything you want, little witch."

You.

***

My hands are shaking again while I light my candle. It's a different shake than the nauseating nerves of last time. There are nerves involved, but they mix with excitement and the desperate edge of my desire.

Gideon's hand wraps around the match again, but this time he presses his naked body into mine, kissing my cheek while he lights his candle. We light the center candle. I can't keep from moaning when his hand comes up from around my waist and squeezes my breast just hard enough that a spike of heat travels down my body.

"Now don't get distracted, little witch."

I bite my lip at Gideon's chastisement, and we blow the match out together. The action that was sensual before is now so intimate that I have to wet my lips. I've done this ritual before, with so many different people, and it's never felt like this. Like our commitment spans years instead of mere hours.

I lean back harder into Gideon's embrace as he starts to toy with my nipple. The flesh of it getting stiffer with each pinch; my breath stuttering with each tug.

"You have something to confess to me, Rose."

I sigh as his teeth scrape over the skin of my throat, hitting the chain of my necklace. I've stalled for long enough. *Be brave, Rose!*

I hum before turning to face him. His eyes are dark and hungry. I can only hope that my request doesn't ruin everything.

"I saw a couple of the regulars—no, that doesn't matter, I want you to take me like… you want something from me. Like you need me." *Like you're claiming me.* I can't say those words though. My heart holds them back.

Gideon frowns slightly. "And you didn't feel that way before?"

I exhale. "I think maybe I'm explaining it wrong." I finger the necklace around my neck, the one that prevents pregnancy. "What if I took this off?"

Make the physical act of claiming a primal one, if not an emotional one that can last forever.

The recognition hits Gideon and he widens his eyes.

I start to back pedal. "Like… a game."

Gideon's hard cock throbs against me. Despite the evidence of his arousal, his brow furrows. "A game?"

"Is that too much? It's just you said you wanted that, and I thought that maybe we could…" I don't even have the words because this wouldn't be a game, or if it were, it would be one with, while unlikely, real consequences.

"Are you saying you want me to try and breed you?" Gideon's voice comes out like a growl and my skin feels too hot to touch. But he's frowning.

Could he be hurt by my request? A throb of clarity cuts through my arousal. Gods, he'd given me his vulnerability that first night, and now I've asked him to try to do the thing he's always wanted and has never been able to accomplish. All because I want to be claimed by him. Hot shame clogs my throat.

"Sorry, gods, I'm being insensitive. Forget I said anything."

I move to step back, but Gideon's arms come around me, pressing his erection harder against me.

Gideon clears his throat. "Rose, stop." His voice sounds rough and he clears his throat again. "I'm far from unwilling, but while I told you that kraken haven't had children, there is always the possibility of… a miracle. It wouldn't be safe to have sex without your protection."

The shame that tightened my throat recedes. I haven't hurt him. *Far from unwilling.*

"What if that'd be a welcome miracle?" Risky. This is all so risky.

But Gideon suggested that he wanted to have a longer relationship than our agreement and I'd always wanted children. If we stayed together, maybe infertility would be something we'd mourn together.

And if a miracle happens and this whole thing does turn to ashes, then at least I'd have something to remember this man by.

Gideon's nostrils flare. "You'd welcome me filling you over and over just for the small chance that something takes root?"

Unmerciful heat flows through me as I nod.

Gideon presses his forehead to mine; the touch is achingly perfect. "Say it, little witch."

"Yes," I breathe.

CHAPTER 17

ROSE

Gideon's arms squeeze me tighter, the hold reminds me of the greedy way his tentacles wrap around me when he partially shifts. He eases the hold and takes a step back.

"Take off the charm, Rose."

The command in his voice has me panting. I do as I'm told. My lower body is heavy and achy. Even the touch of fingers on my skin to get to the clasp of the chain are like small drags of a tongue. While I'm trying to open the clasp I watch Gideon's hands fist and flex, as if he's trying to keep from snatching me up and having his wicked way with me.

Even with how primed his body is, how hard his cock, Gideon's mouth is a stern line. Concern banks my arousal.

"Are you sure you want to do this? You don't look happy."

Gideon huffs. "I'm trying to figure out how to keep from pinning you to the bedding and rutting you like an animal. Give me a moment."

His voice is raspy and forceful.

"I'm not opposed to being taken like an animal."

Gideon's body tenses and he looks up at the ceiling. The man swallows before he speaks again. "You need to come first."

"I'm also not opposed to that." A playfulness edges into my voice now that Gideon seems to be trying to slow this interaction and a rough sound escapes him, making me jump.

"Don't!—Don't run, Rose."

I blink as things become clear. Gideon is an apex predator and I've just offered up a helluva primal incentive.

"Okay, maybe you can chase me later." I place my necklace in a dish on the altar and the sound of the metal clinking against glass echoes. The vulnerability of not wearing the charm amps up the moment. I've never had sex without that charm. Never wanted to take the risk with anyone else until now.

Something about Gideon makes this feel right.

"Tease." Gideon's chest swells at that and he glares. "Touch yourself for me, little witch."

I stand awkwardly a few feet from him. "Um, here?"

I move as if I'm going to go to the bedding and Gideon flinches. I halt before slowly walking backward instead. Gideon follows me, so careful to leave the space between us. I press back against the tiled wall. The chill of the stone spreads goose bumps across my skin. No escape.

"I thought I was going to feel your mouth on me?"

Gideon shakes his head. "We start this way. Later, I'll fuck you with my tongue until you beg me to stop. Right now, touch yourself. Show me what you like, Rose."

I lean back, breath shallow, and run a hand up my body to my breast to squeeze it teasingly for his gaze. Gideon had looked tense before. Now the muscles strain under his skin in a way that has my hips shifting.

"Your cunt, Rose. Show me how wet you are. Show me how much you want my cock and maybe I'll give it to you."

The intensity of this interaction swirls between us; the pull makes me want to lean in and give myself to Gideon. But the dangerous way he watches me has my lizard brain reacting, pulling back, increasing my heart rate so I can flee. Gideon's eyes flash, as if he can hear the ways that my body wants to betray my mind. He probably can.

I press my hand to myself and new embarrassment fills me at how wet I am. My fingers slide through my folds with no resistance and Gideon groans at my weak whimper.

"Fuck, you're so wet." Gideon's cheeks flag red and he wets his lips. "Show me."

I set my foot on a convenient side pillow and open my legs. I bite my lip, swearing that I can feel Gideon's exhale hitting my wetness.

"Such a pretty cunt, I can't wait until I can see my cum dripping from it. Is that what's gotten you so hot, little witch? Have you been spending hours thinking about how I'm going to fill you up? How desperately I'm going to take you?"

My exhale is shaky and I softly circle my clit. "Gods, yes."

"How many times can I have you tonight?"

I pant even as Gideon asks about logistics. "I mean, there's some healing salve, so…"

I jump at Gideon's sharp curse and squeak at the too hard stroke I give my clit.

"Use your fingers, little witch. Stretch yourself so you're ready for me."

I huff even as I slide a finger into myself and shiver at the penetration, pressing myself harder against the wall. "I'm getting sick of doing all the work. If I wanted to masturbate, why would I need you?"

A small smile curves across Gideon's mouth.

"This way I can be sure that you orgasm first. That's important to me, I don't know how much I'll be able to think about that when you're hot around me." The smile disappears. "When I know I'm breeding you."

Fuck, it's hot when he says that. It must be the deviant part of me that lives for reducing this strategic man to a rutting beast. I make a sound that has Gideon tensing again and I slide another finger in, trying to ready myself as much as I can while this primal feeling courses through me.

"I'll come when you're inside me." I don't think I could stop myself.

"And you think you're ready for my cock, little witch?"

I nod and slide my fingers from myself impatiently. Gideon is so rigid that anticipation sparks and I'd tell him I was ready even if I wasn't already soaked with wanting. I step toward him and stop at the fierce look on his face.

Gideon's eyes are so dark that I shiver. A stillness falls over us before he breaks it.

"Run."

That word skitters over my skin and hesitation spikes through me before I turn and sprint mindlessly. It's lucky that my fight-or-flight instinct starts me running toward the bedding because Gideon's body hits me quickly. I cry out as we both go down into the pillows and generous padding.

Gideon's body is hot against my skin and surrounds me. Instinct still drives my motions as I struggle under the hold keeping his front to my back. He stills but keeps me tight in his grasp.

Gideon snarls and I freeze.

"Sorry." His voice is hoarse, and the instinctual panic recedes even as I breathe hard.

"It took me by surprise." I tremble, adrenaline still flowing through me. Gideon nips the nape of my neck before licking me, tasting me. I rest my forehead to the bed and breathe out slowly. Gods, he feels amazing wrapped around me.

"I'll tell you if I need to stop," I say. "But please, please don't stop."

It's the right thing to say.

He grunts behind me and presses his erection decadently against my ass. The wet smears against me. "That begging you do makes it hard to say no to anything. If you say the word, I'd give you everything."

A small sound escapes my mouth at that. The craving to do just that, to beg to keep him, rings through my bones. I bite my lip to keep from spilling that into this heated moment. That discussion will happen later.

Gideon's body moves. My mind trips over his grip on my hip and the pull of my body upward until his thickness slides through my slick folds. My hands clutch the sheets of the bedding.

I gasp as he mounts me, the head of his cock smoothly slides into me with little pressure and I moan as Gideon tunnels the rest of his cock into my depths with a surge of his hips.

I'm as ready as I could have been, but it's still a stretch. I tense around his cock and bask in the satisfying fullness.

"Oh, Rose." Gideon's voice sounds worshiping. "You own me."

Everything in me yields at that. He might say I own him, but it's me that gives. It's an utter surrender. I'm

Gideon Strand's, my body, my heart, he has my very soul if he ever asks for it. Hell, he might not even have to ask for it.

My face is pressed into the sheets when the first thrust comes. The abrupt motion is jarring but completes me at the same time. By the second thrust, I push back into it, welcoming Gideon into me with enthusiasm.

He grunts as our bodies smack together. "You'll take my cock and work for my seed to fill you up, won't you?"

Gideon grips my hair and the pull of it, knowing he can make me take whatever he gives me, has my mouth opening.

"*Yes, yes, yes.*"

"Mine." The pronouncement is guttural, and he hisses when I clench around him.

"Please, Gideon."

The lights might flicker, or my mind is short-circuiting because he pounds into my accepting body. His motions drive the waves of sensation higher and higher until I'm gasping and my climax rushes through me. When I cry out, Gideon buries his erection deep with a violent groan. His hot release bathes my insides.

Gideon clutches me tightly, pulsing more of his cum into me, and I sigh from the bliss of it.

I relax onto the bedding and stretch my arms and legs. Gideon's weight is still on top of me and I savor the sensation of security, of belonging. His mouth drops lazy kisses on the dewy skin of my shoulder. As if I'm a precious thing to be coddled.

I hum at the tickle. "Gods, that was wonderful."

Gideon smiles against my skin and his erection throbs inside me. I jolt in response, my eyes fluttering closed with a sigh. Gideon's arm wraps lower around my stomach, tilting my hips up before he moves inside me again.

A sound of surprise escapes me at the gentle rock of him. The wind down of my body starts to reverse and my eyes pop open.

"H-how are you still hard?" I ask as another rock of our bodies together threatens to have me start babbling again. Every movement is a delicious friction.

"I told you I'm more magic than anything else." Gideon's words sound teasing but the primal nature of him still emanates underneath. He scrapes his teeth across my shoulder. "It's a small thing to keep an erection if I want it."

Unlike the frenzied mating of before, our motions stay slow. The drag of him inside me paired with the heat of his body cradling mine has a whimper building at the back of my throat. Little by little, my body tightens with each gentle rock. With each inciting word that falls from Gideon's lips.

"My beautiful little witch, my perfect treasure, you take me so well. I could fill you for days and still need to hold you."

I don't notice my tears until he's wiping them away with a shushing sound. Everything is just so much, my emotions rock in time to our bodies.

"You make my three hearts beat," Gideon teases.

My laugh is a choked sound, and my throat is thick. "Please don't leave me."

I don't mean to say the words. I don't even register them until Gideon's chest rumbles with a chuckle against my back. "Oh, little witch, I couldn't leave you even if you wanted me to."

He laces his fingers through mine and squeezes as his other arm releases my waist, he doesn't need to tilt my hips anymore, I do that myself, needing the deep penetration of his body into mine. His free hand reaches under me, fingers circling my clit, pressing just hard enough that I cry out.

"That's it, Rose. Come for me, let it happen. I want your body to suck me in and never let go."

Gideon plays my body like the simplest instrument in existence. Every touch tuned to the demanded reaction and soon the small motions of him inside me aren't enough. I tighten around him, greedily needing everything and getting just enough to drive my pleasure higher with each careful motion.

"Please, Gideon, please I need—"

"You need to come for me, sweet treasure. You need to scream my name." Gideon's words are deceptively calm, but the dark power of him plucks at the tight strings of my body and I do exactly what he says. The climax roars through me like the deadliest storm. I scream and thrash, unable to move much in the grip of my kraken. Each crash of my senses drives me higher and I do cry out his name.

Gideon thrusts harshly into me then, breaking his measured pace with a snarl, filling my body again with his release. I sob and gasp at the perfection.

The singing perfection lasts the space of a couple breaths before I return to my sweaty overheated body, weighed down and cradled by a gasping Gideon.

Air, I need air.

I clumsily tap Gideon. The first time he pushed me to orgasm, his weight was reassuring. The second time, I need to catch my breath.

Gideon rolls us onto our sides, and I slide his cock from me with a wince.

"I'll—" He pants. "I'll get the salve."

I mumble something, I'm not even sure what, as Gideon slowly sits up. It's a tiny bit gratifying to sap the strength of an ancient being that could crush me.

I flop onto my back and pull Gideon down. My nails dig into his shoulders, but he lets me drag him, sensing my intention. His mouth drops to mine and the kiss is slow, a hazy dream unfolding into a measured, luxurious tasting before I break it to gasp in more air and let him leave the bed.

My heart starts to slow back to a normal rhythm by the time he returns and breaks open the container. I'm more grateful than I've ever been that Lowell convinced us to splurge on the salves and lube available to clients. Instead of an antiseptic smell, the scent of roses hits me, and I smile like a fool.

"It's like it was made just for me."

Gideon smiles at my silliness and eases my legs apart.

"Your cunt dripping from me is the most satisfying picture." He hums. "Some base part of me wants to close your legs and let my seed soak inside you, but the rest knows that that's ridiculous."

My breath catches and, somehow, I'm still able to blush when Gideon gently massages the salve between my legs. He watches my face closely as he pushes two fingers into me, spreading the salve internally and rubbing circles against my G-spot. My body perks up as he presses harder.

"Really?" I whisper, exasperated at myself.

Gideon's eyes crinkle. "You seem to like it."

I huff, but spread my legs wider. I'm surprised at my hunger, this all-consuming want. My breath catches at the look of satisfaction on Gideon's face as this impossible man tugs another orgasm to the surface. My back arches and I'm shouting to the stars in the sky.

"Oh gods, no more." I close my legs and Gideon lets me, dropping a kiss to my knee.

"Now it's time to feed you."

CHAPTER 18

GIDEON

"Oh gods, oh yes. Just like that—" Rose breaks off on a moan and I raise a brow, continuing to massage her lower back under the water. Digging into a muscle near her spine just how she wants.

My body reacts to the sounds she makes, but satisfaction makes the urge easy to suppress.

A happy glow has taken the place of my weary, dark heart and I wouldn't be surprised if I were smiling. My face is starting to hurt. I'm not a male that smiles often but being with Rose settles something in me. Some scrabbling, ravenous thing that urges me to seek, to hunt, to find.

I wonder if I was meant to find her all along.

Rose sighs and tilts her head back against my shoulder. I nip her throat, making her laugh. The pizza was satisfying in the way only cheesy carbs can be and my mate languishes under my hands.

I'm happy. So content that I don't even want to move. I just want to keep this woman in my arms always, but curiosity bites at me.

"So, what brought up wanting to be bred?"

Rose bites her lips bashfully before answering.

"It was a couple that regularly comes in. The public pools usually have some magnificent exhibitionist displays." She hums in thought. "He was just so determined, almost like he wanted to claim her on another level, a primal one. That got me thinking of how being the focus of that kind of energy would feel. And... I like you. I wanted to be with you in a way I've never been with anyone else."

I raise my brows again, but Rose continues on a rush.

"Don't get me wrong, the tentacles are unique, but that only required my consent. I wanted an active role in something that sets our experience apart. A moment that I was brave with you."

All this smiling is dangerous for me. I pull Rose closer on my lap, creating waves in the bathing pool as I kiss the damp curls on the back of her neck.

"It was... like nothing I've ever experienced. I'll admit I lost control of myself a little bit when you offered yourself up so nicely. Even if nothing comes of it, it's an experience I'll hold close to my heart for the rest of my days. Thank you, Rose."

Rose stiffens and I'm confused to why until she speaks. "Rest of your days. So forever?"

"Unless someone shortens that span."

"What it must be like to be immortal."

There's an abrupt coldness in me. I've been what I am for thousands of years, I forget sometimes that others don't have my lifespan. It's a silly thing to slip my mind since it seems to be a subject Rose has thought about.

How very sloppy of you, Gideon. I've been so focused on trying to catch my mate that I didn't consider how our life would look together. I ease the tightness in my chest. I'll figure this out. There would be ways to form some kind of bond between us.

And if there isn't a way for her to gain immortality, there will be ways to do away with mine.

I won't lose Rose after just finding her.

"Nothing is a guarantee, little witch. My lifespan is something we can figure out—"

Rose pulls away and I cut my words off. Frustration burns in me at how quickly we're back to careful words about the future.

"I should probably head home if we're done for the night," Rose says. She turns toward me but won't meet my gaze.

My witch is attempting to run away from me. After everything we've shared.

I wish I were a mind reader so I could reassure every concern that she has, but I'm not. I can only be strategic and patient.

I will catch my mate.

"I wouldn't say we're done. Are you done?" I run my fingertips up her body and Rose's stiffness fades on a shiver.

"I… don't have to be done." Rose's words are hesitant, as if she knows I'm weaving seduction to keep her with me, but can't help herself from giving in.

My smile is sharp and I pull her back to me, to straddle me in the water. My hands rove her body, bestowing soft touches that have Rose's breath going shallow.

"My m—" I stop and mentally curse myself for almost slipping the word *mate* into our play for the second time tonight. I catch her mouth with mine, savoring the feel of her lips before breaking the kiss. "Stay with me, Rose?"

She squirms as my thumb runs through her folds and circles her clit.

"O-okay, but I'm a little sensitive," she says.

I hum, softening the strokes of my thumb. No stretching then, but there's more I can do to seduce my mate. I move before she second-guesses her agreement and lift her from the water, setting her on the edge of the bathing pool. The water runs down her pale skin and I have the urge to lick up every drop trail, but I'm craving something else.

I arrange some waterproof cushions around her. Rose frowns at me when I lean her back. I drop lower into the water, between her legs.

"Gideon, what are you—oh gods."

My tongue strokes over Rose's folds before any more of her sense returns; the sense that tells her to keep me at a distance. Her response is guttural and satisfying. I groan at the burst of her flavor on my tongue and her fingers dig into my hair, pulling me away for a breath.

"Wh-what are you doing? I thought you wanted to play breed-the-willing-witch?"

I snort, appreciating the name. "I told you that I'd taste you later. Well, actually I said I'd tongue fuck you until you begged me to stop if my memory serves me."

Rose whimpers but spreads her legs wider. I grin, enjoying that she isn't going to reject this action or tell me that I don't need to do it. My cock aches but it's a distant sensation, compared to tasting my mate. I stroke my tongue through her wetness, lightly at first.

Her taste is delicate and tart, accented by the rose healing salve and mixes satisfyingly well with the taste of myself. I suck and lick at turns, reading the ways Rose's body squirms and tenses as she pants for me, before stopping to tease.

"Any complaints?"

"No complaints!" Rose gasps.

I work her over slowly, not pushing to climax, but through softly breaking waves of pleasure. It's a delicate process, and with each stroke Rose loses a little more composure. The skin over her beautiful breasts flushes to match her cheeks. Her fingers clasp my hair, erotically pulling it when she forgets herself.

I know the exact moment I've lost control of my shift.

The world shines a little brighter, shadows disappear and the taste on my tongue bursts with clarity. My lower half spreads out in the water with searching tentacles. One limb searching for a particular place, wanting to bind, to mate, to fill.

I almost don't realize I've wrapped tentacles around each of Rose's legs, from ankle to knee, until she cries out in surprise.

"Oh gods, I love that," she says.

The tentacles spread her legs wider without a thought from me. My mating tentacle strokes up through her folds, matching the actions of my tongue, but not penetrating.

I lift my face to make eye contact. "Will you accept my seed like this, Rose? I'll be gentle."

Gently fill her with the fluids my creature wants to see drip from her again. Mating with a tentacle isn't the same as a cock, it's a continuous process that takes time.

"You can come inside me with the—? Yes, please!"

I groan as my tentacle disappears inside Rose's pink folds. The creature in me pushes it to go deeper, deep enough to coil and stop the seed from flowing out. Rose moves her hips as if to fuck herself with the intrusion.

My body shudders, my seed fills my mate.

Rose lurches upward. "Whoa!"

I press against her stomach, my tentacles on her legs tighten, to keep her from moving.

"That's more *stuff* than I expected." Rose's cheeks are a pink that deepens to red as, despite my best intentions, my seed spills out around my mating tentacle.

Already the creature needs to replace the loss and pleasure shivers through me.

Rose whimpers, her body clutching onto me as if embarrassed as more of me spills from her.

"So damn beautiful," I say.

"Oh gods, Gideon, I didn't know it was going to be like this."

That freezes me. "Do you want to stop?"

"No! It's just so much fluid… it's hot, but I'm making a mess."

I chuckle. "It's more accurate to say that I'm the one making the mess. The next spurts will be less, I promise."

Rose's eyes are wide. "This is… is this… coming like this is a ongoing process?" Her head falls back. "Of course it is."

And then she laughs, the sound musical. "I should have watched more Discovery Channel."

I smile but drop my head again. Rose is entirely too levelheaded right now for my liking. Her moan at my tongue on her brings another shiver through me. I pulse inside her, sucking on her clit as an orgasm has her shouting.

I bring her down to drive her back up again, she begs and prays to the old gods throughout.

The night goes on with me driving up Rose's pleasure with every lick and suck. The feel of her, the *need* to mate, brings more releases from me. In the end, I coil more of my tentacle inside her, letting our combined fluids spill out from the pressure, and she breaks beautifully.

I cradle her after, wanting to say all the words.

That she's a treasure, that she amazes me, and that I want her to be mine forever.

As it is, I only say the first two, even as the truth of the third burns in my chest.

I try, instead, to use my actions to say the words that I can't yet voice.

***

Another day of waking up next to Rose. I'd worn her out the night before and when I teased her about leaving the bathhouse, she had scowled grumpily at me and pulled me in to cuddle her on the bedding. Triumph is sweet.

"What are you thinking about?" Rose asks. Her voice is husky with sleep, and I want to wear her out all over again, but that isn't happening.

"I didn't realize you were awake."

I run a hand over her hair, appreciating the fiery glints that reflect the lights of the slow-burning candles.

"Don't think I can't tell when you're avoiding my questions," she says. There's no heat in her words.

"The auction that Mace and I are taking down is scheduled for tonight. I probably won't get to see you again until tomorrow."

She hums. "I'll survive. A night to let the salve really work would be good."

Rose's tone has a mischievous air and I'm at ease. My mate will wait for me.

"Something else." I clench my teeth for a pause but continue when Rose frowns in concern. "Since it's going to be riskier than we planned. I just need—" I consider my words. This is not something I'm willing to fumble. "I need you to keep your distance. There are so many wards around this building that it's safe, but I'll be able to focus better if you agree to keep away from it."

Rose wrinkles her nose.

"Will you be at risk?"

I snort. "No."

I've been liberating paranormals since the practice first began. I'll be fine, but I'm unwilling to put Rose in danger.

"Gideon, I'm not helpless. But I'll keep my distance if it helps you feel better. It shouldn't be hard; I've had no reason to visit that store before." Rose yawns and buries her face into my chest.

Relief soothes the worst of my worries. I wait for Rose to ask me questions about the situation. And wait. But her body doesn't tense with curiosity.

Odd.

It's a surprise that Rose doesn't bring up the trafficking happening next door. That she doesn't seem interested in interrogating me about it. There are many paranormals that are isolationists and don't involve themselves in these matters, but that doesn't seem like Rose.

Perhaps she's just tired? She and Lowell worked through the other night on the wards.

Perhaps it is a combination of reasons, but I hesitate to bring up such an ugly thing in this happy space if she doesn't want to discuss it.

It won't matter anyway, Mace and I will take out the auction hosts and stop the event before it even starts.

I will protect my mate.

I kiss her head, her hair smells of the spicy aroma of the room, it settles me. "I put all the details you need in that email, but text me if you have any concerns."

Rose mumbles her assent and something about her inbox before popping her head up. "Can we get breakfast? I burned through a lot of energy last night."

Triumph and joy fill me. My strategy is working. This witch is mine. Now, I just need to figure out a way to keep her.

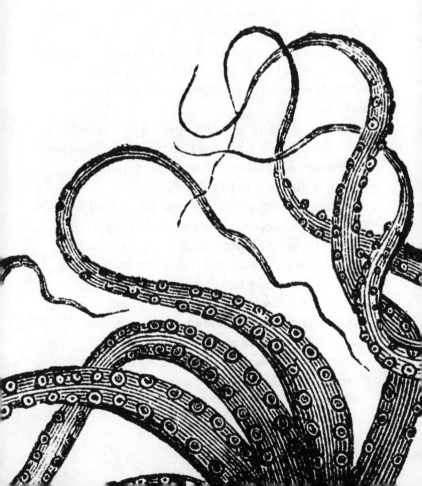

CHAPTER 19

ROSE

I hum cheerfully as I connect names on my textured stationery. The light of the lamp hits the octopus engraving of my *courting* gift and scatters charming flecks of gold across my desk. The pink stone pen matches beautifully with the marbled gray paper with a metallic gold border.

The drag of the ink on paper sparks a joy in me that is hard to deny myself. I'd gotten into the habit of denying myself since Jackson. I'm glad to break from it now.

What is life if not to be enjoyed?

Shaking me from my funk is something that I'll always be grateful to Gideon for. No matter what happens—

Nope! I refuse to waste time dwelling on how this relationship with Gideon will end, or our incompatible lifespans. We could be together for the next twenty years. I'm not going to shortchange us by worrying about something as permanent as immortality right when I'm finally hitting my stride again.

I match an *Amelia Lavender* to a *Luke Grant* with a flourish. My sigh is gusty and satisfied. I've been struggling with their profiles for weeks. As it has in the past, the flow of ink and quill lets my mind wander.

It's a simple form of magic to pluck names and add them to my doodles but the more I look at them the more sense it makes.

Amelia and Luke both come from large witch families, are invested in their careers, and don't want children. I'd rate their soul compatibility at a solid fifty percent. They both moved out of their multigenerational family homes recently and I'm willing to bet that they sought out matching to deal with the new loneliness of it.

For the first time in months, I don't agonize over the numbers.

I'm more aware than ever that soul compatibility isn't everything. I'll disclose my reasons for the match and let the couple sort out the details. My only responsibility is to offer people options, it's up to a couple to keep from getting heartbroken.

It's as if a particularly ugly stain that had soaked into the very threads of my being has been rinsed away. I was stuck, and now I'm not.

And tomorrow I'll see Gideon. Tomorrow we'll discuss what kind of longer lasting arrangement we are each interested in and I will be brave. Fear of heartbreak will not cheat me out of happiness; in part, because I already know I'll be heartbroken when whatever we have together ends. I'm already invested even if I haven't pulled the proverbial trigger yet.

I finish writing the emails to Amelia and Luke, notifying them of the match, before going to my inbox. It's an utter mess. I get at least a hundred emails a day; hopefuls reach out to me from all over the world. Many matches are easy ones, as simple as pulling out another candidate from where I sorted them. Sorting candidates that I don't have matches readily available for takes up most of my day, and then the rest of the day is devoted to following up with matches and other communications.

I try to stay on top of it but sometimes it can take a week before I get to an email. My clients are always warned of the delay, they know matching can take time. I scroll through the unread emails and one catches my eye.

An email from *Gideon Strand* and I smile to myself. The giddiness I get from reading his name in my inbox is a little ridiculous, but I embrace it. He did mention something about an email this morning.

I open it.

As I read, the smile falls from my face in small degrees. Nauseating anger kindles instead. The auction hosts next door are trafficking *people*. Why didn't Gideon say anything about this when we were together? Did he just assume I'd read the email?

That he suspects that the hosts might also be responsible for the magic drain feels small in comparison to the act of selling people, but this applies directly to the bathhouse. I forward the email to Jared and call his office.

"What is it, Rose?"

"I just sent you an email from Gideon with a suspect for our magic drain. Jared" —fury makes it hard to speak— "they're selling people next door."

"What?" Jared's voice booms over the line and I pull the phone away, wincing. "Wait, I just opened it… Rose—"

"Oh, he attached a photo of one of the hosts—"

"Rose, don't!"

My heart freezes in my chest when I open the file. In the photo is the man I'd labeled my perfect match, that I'd flung myself at. Bile rises in my throat at the image of an annoyed looking Jackson touching the brick wall of the bathhouse.

Things click, devastatingly, in place. Time slows as each detail starts to tick to life.

Jackson read so compatible to me when I met him because he had been glutted on magic from the very source of mine, the bathhouse. Every spell, every ward, crafted in this building vibrates in cohesive perfection to the Love family. The magic harvested carries our special signature.

He must have been imbibing the raw magic, getting high in an incredibly expensive way.

He had been stealing magic and I hadn't even realized.

"He used me."

"Rose," Jared says. The warning in his voice falls flat. He couldn't stop me on a magical rampage if he tried. Lowell likes to joke that our family are lovers not fighters, but we choose that path because our strengths when used in battle are catastrophic. "I can't imagine that he meant to use you, he'd have no way of knowing that you'd read him as being compatible."

"He stole our magic. The magic built on consensual acts. What if he is using that magic to fund the sale of *people*?" I hiss, but my lips numb on a choked sob.

Our business. Peoples' *lives*. Desecrated.

I've been bloodthirsty a select number of times in my life. Enough to know that the sensation of fiery anger cooling into icy rage requires action. "He won't get away with this."

"Goddammit, Rose, slow down—"

I hang up the phone, my magic thrums under my skin in time to the frenzy of my emotions. How much more magic was Jackson able to steal because I let him in? The man that I shared my body with, that had made me feel small, is guilty of ruining other people's lives.

My thoughts are a spiral, a tumbling stone growing to a boulder, gaining momentum and power with each spin. I leave my office and ignore Lowell's wave. In a blink, I exit the bathhouse. The wind is cutting and cruel today, but it only adds to the swell of rage. I don't bring any tools of magic with me; I don't need any.

I only have the demanding pulse under my skin. An instinct unique to our bloodline from before the bathhouse was opened, when soul threads were used to devastate instead of match.

The demand to serve judgment.

CHAPTER 20

GIDEON

Mace tightens the restraint around the wrist of auction host Mark Dewitt until the man yelps. Either he was stung by the magic bonds or the restraint is too tight, it's a minor discomfort that bothers neither Mace nor me considering the state we'd found the captives. Jackson Dewitt is already bound, arms behind his back, glowering at us from his place on the floor.

"I'm going to pop out and drop this sack of garbage"— Mace gives another tug on Mark's restraints— "off at the local Council before coming back with supplies. We'll have some time until the Council can send representatives to record this event and help these women get back home."

Mace gives me a look. He means that I'll have time with this Jackson character to gain more information. We'd quickly figured out that Mark knows next to nothing, his name on the auction is more as a figurehead. Mark is merely an unfortunate cousin to the real "mastermind" of the operation, probably lured in with promises of the immense profit to be had.

"The Council will probably want to set up an operation to apprehend the attendees of the auction."

We have hours yet until the time the auction is slated for. Mace and I waited for the moment that the hosts transported the "merchandise" to the location to make our move. The tussle had been short and easier than anticipated because the hosts hadn't bothered to hire any extra security.

Two male witches didn't have a hope in hell of besting a demon and a kraken.

The lack of security stinks of this being a quick cash grab and I wonder who these men owe money to.

The auction had been planned to occur in the basement of the store. I'd have preferred we stay in that more secure location until we tied up loose ends, but the women were uneasy with staying in an enclosed space with no windows, next to magic cages intended for them.

I don't blame them.

Now the five women held captive lean against the dusty antiques of the store. The clothing they wear ranges from transparent fabrics to grubby pajamas on the individuals too powerful to risk forcing to dress in a certain way. They all have suppression collars on to keep them from accessing any magical abilities they have. I itch to rip the collars off, but past experience tells me it's better to wait until the women feel more secure in their surroundings.

Fragile like a bomb is an apt saying for the situation.

One of them had found a stack of moth-eaten quilts in the store and they're all bundled up, watching Mace's and my actions with blank stares.

"To set up an operation would be a logical choice for the Council." It's all I have to say. Mace rolls his eyes in silent agreement that the Council doesn't always make logical choices.

Our distrust of the Council is why I'm going to interrogate this Jackson character before the Council comes and takes him into custody. He has a mental guest list of interested buyers and contacts that have somehow enslaved these paranormal beings for a profit.

I don't want to ponder how long some of these women have been imprisoned.

Just considering it makes my nature writhe. It's taking a good amount of self-control to keep from ripping the head off this cretin. How many times has he done this before? This was the first auction at this location, but most locations were only used for a short amount of time before the Council swooped in and shut them down.

I take some grim satisfaction that within the last hundred years the auctions have transitioned from grand affairs to small scratched-out dives. It's not enough.

The issue of clearing out the rot of slavery is frustratingly persistent. It should be as simple as making the trade illegal, but there are old holdouts. Powerful shadow figures heading the operations, waiting for the Council to lose power or for people to stop caring.

Mace teleports with Mark, and I'm left with the women and Jackson. I pull the pathetic man off the floor by his mussed dress shirt, enjoying the sound of the expensive fabric ripping in my grip.

"So, Jack, what is it going to take for you to tell me who you're working with?"

Jackson's eyes shift back and forth.

"I'll tell you if you let me go."

A whimper escapes one of the women and I take a breath. I hide my rage behind a mask of politeness.

"Let's just pretend for a minute that was an option for you. How could I trust you to tell me all the players in this game, if you know you'll have to run from them? No, I think the safest place for you is a Council holding cell."

"You think they can't reach me in a Council cell?" Jackson hisses before breaking into a harsh laugh. "I'll be dead by the end of the week."

"Well," I say as if I'm mulling the whole thing over. "It sounds like it's in your interest to tell me exactly who you're afraid to anger—"

There's a crash at the front of the store and frustration rises. The front door was locked.

I prepare myself to face the unknown foe and almost stumble at the sight of Rose. My Rose. Vibrating with a violence I've never seen from her.

"Rose, what are you doing here?"

Rose looks at me with some surprise before her gaze takes in the women wrapped in quilts and her magic surges like claws across my skin. *Who is this woman?*

Jackson scoffs, ignorant to the power filling the room. "You two know each other? Let me guess, she's fucked you, right?"

I blink, trying to catch up with the dynamics playing in front of me and not snarl at his tone.

"You used me," Rose says. Her voice sounds throttled.

Jackson laughs. "Don't flatter yourself. You weren't a part of the plan, just showed up on one of the visits I took to finalize the drain. Saying I was your *perfect match* with your legs spread."

The words are ugly, and I see each one hit in the way my mate's shoulders rise and tense.

"This is your ex?" I ask, mentally deducing at the rate of molasses, but when I do, the rage I'd banked takes on a new life. This is the man that put that shattered look on Rose's face. That destroyed her confidence. This man is why I've had to stalk my mate with patience and earn her trust.

He hurt her.

Jackson starts gasping before I even realize my hand is around his throat, but in the space of two breaths I remember why he can't die yet and release him. Everyone in the room jumps at the sound of anger I emit.

"You will go into Council custody. If you say a single thing like that again, to anyone, I will break you first."

Rose walks forward, animosity coming off her in waves. "No! It's not enough. His family will just pull strings and get him out."

"Rose—" I step in front of Jackson and flinch at the snap of her power. It would seem as if my Rose has some thorns I didn't know about. Admiration stirs, but I try to tamp it down and focus on the situation.

"Don't try and stop me!" she says.

"He needs to stand trial. He has information we require. Information to take down the people in charge of this operation, so that this doesn't happen again."

Rose takes in the women again. "He used magic from the bathhouse for *this*." Her voice cracks. "He hurt people."

The bathhouse is a safe place for sexual encounters of all kinds, I can understand why she's so upset with its system being perverted for this purpose, even if it was through theft. It doesn't change that I can't just let Rose do whatever she plans on doing.

"I'm sorry, Rose, but we need him alive."

Rose takes a step back, as if my words are finally landing as they should. The currents of energy she's giving off in waves start to lull and I breathe a sigh of relief.

"Please." The voice is so small we almost miss it, but Rose's head snaps up to the speaker.

My heart breaks at the sight of one of the women stumbling forward. Getting too close to the action for my tastes. I've lost a potential witness before when a group of freed paranormals decided to tear him apart and fell upon the both of us.

I didn't lose any sleep at the man's death, but the incident is the main reason the collars stay on now.

The woman's blank face has been replaced with a one stretched with distress. She's much younger than the others, maybe not even eighteen. She's been wearing the collar for so long I can't get any sense of what kind of paranormal she is.

"He said he'd kill my family unless I did everything he said. I d-don't want anything to happen to them. Or for them to be taken too. I have s-sisters, one is only three." Tears run down the teenager's face and all the reasons I have for standing in the way of Rose's vengeance weaken. I want to kill this man, even if doing so would cause a hassle with the Council.

For an organization that isn't as useful as it should be, they don't take to vigilante justice well.

But this girl deserves to feel safe.

Rose takes in a deep breath "What's your name?"

"Corey."

"Corey, Jackson will get what's coming to him. I promise you he'll pay. But—" Rose sighs. "Gideon says they need information from him to stop others from suffering how you've suffered."

Suspicion creases my brow. I expected Rose to demand me to let her destroy this monster. I know I want to.

"Y-you said that his family would get him out."

Now Rose looks embarrassed. The energy she mustered in her anger still hangs in the air, but I can see her coming

back to herself. Perhaps she's beginning to experience
the energy drain witches do if they use large amounts of
magic at once.

"That might have been a little dramatic of me to say.
They're more likely to disown him since he has a brother.
Isn't that right, Jackson? Yeah, I bet your family will leave
you out to dry, you creep."

Rose glares at Jackson, who sneers at her.

Corey takes another step closer and I tense, keeping
an eye on her hands which clutch the blanket with white
knuckles. But the teen just lifts her chin.

"You promise?"

"I'll see to it myself." Rose's voice is grim.

For some reason Corey seems to believe her. It isn't
just Corey, it's all the women. It has to be the energy Rose
permeates the room with because the blank stares are now
replaced with a variety of expressions from surliness to
fierce anger.

My mate is amazing.

I begin to turn to fully face Jackson, we still only have
until the Council officials show up to get the information
we need, when he bursts into motion.

Jackson reaches past me with a magical level of speed
and snatches Corey by the arm, grabbing the collar around
her throat. The girl lets out a wail that cuts off. Rose and I
freeze.

"It's tuned to him," Rose mutters.

I clench my jaw. The suppression collars must be
Jackson's personal magic. The restraints that would
have suppressed his magic lie on the floor, somehow
deactivated. Jackson can cause Corey pain and even her
death if this is handled poorly.

"Very smart, Rose. Now, you two are going to let me leave." Jackson juts his chin up, gesturing us back. "Or your little friend will experience greater pain than she has before."

Jackson's cheek twitches and Corey whimpers.

"You aren't taking her," Rose says.

Jackson scoffs. "I don't think you have any say in the situation."

"Take me instead."

My inner beast roars at that, but I push the rage down. I extend my magic out to surround Jackson, invisible until the moment it gets into position. I won't let him take Rose or Corey.

Jackson's lip curls in disgust. "You? You're not worth anything. No, I'll keep this captive. Now, get out of my way."

Rose takes a step forward and Corey screams. Rose stumbles back.

I'm not in position to act when the tables turn.

I'm so focused on Jackson and Corey, that it happens in a blink. As one, the women attack Jackson. Using inventory from the defunct antique shop and swinging with rage. Jackson loses his grip on Corey as items rain down on him. A golf club, a sterling silver jewelry box, and a particularly vicious looking saxophone beat down on Jackson.

Corey sobs, but moves out of reach while Rose and I rush forward. To do what? It's unclear. Who am I to stand between these women and their form of justice?

Jackson bellows in rage and all the women drop to the floor. My stomach drops. *The collars.* He must be using the last of his reserves to control them all at once.

"No!" Rose cries.

I grab Jackson's arms, ready to slap another restraint on the man when my gentle, fierce witch grabs Jackson's face.

Waves of energy disturb the air around us, crackling with static and winding inward. Jackson starts to seize and choke but Rose doesn't release his face.

"You will hurt no one else," she says.

The words reverberate with power and the hairs on my body stand on end. Jackson screams but the sound cuts off when whatever Rose is casting collapses around him.

The tension in Jackson's body goes lax and the shop drops into silence, only disrupted by the sounds of the women pushing themselves up. Rose's hands fall from Jackson's face and her step backward is loud against the laminate. I stand, pulling along Jackson, who is conscious... but blank.

I blink at Jackson's face and he blinks at me. All the rage, sneers, and ugliness are gone. It's as if all his emotions have been wiped away. It's eerie.

"Well, I seem to have missed the excitement."

As a group, we turn. Mace holds a box bursting with water bottles and different color sweats. Right, the supplies he mentioned. My friend doesn't fidget under the stares.

Mace gives a dry smile. "Anyone feeling like a protein bar?"

Surprisingly, it's Corey that pops up and nears the demon first. "Are they gross flavors?"

Mace lifts an eyebrow. "They're protein bars. What do you think?"

The teen coughs in what might be a laugh and Mace hands over the supplies. "Distribute these, will you? I need to talk to my partner."

Corey nods and glances at Rose. "You made him pay."

Rose nods. "I did. He won't do anything to your family now. He can't."

Mace clears his throat. "Is everyone okay?"

"I think so," I say, taking stock of the women who nod and wearily watch Jackson. "I just don't know how he got free."

Rose gives a humorless laugh. "His wrists have tattoos that a school friend did on a bet. He bragged that no restraints could hold him. I thought it was an exaggeration."

"The tattoos work." Jackson's monotone voice makes everyone jump.

Everyone but Mace, that is. Mace closes the distance to Jackson and examines him. The demon gives a whistle, impressed.

"Is this your work?" he asks Rose.

Rose swallows. "He should be able to answer questions, and probably in more of an agreeable way."

"I've only seen a soul binding a few times… and never from a witch. Good job."

I straighten. *A soul binding?* No wonder energy had come off Rose in waves. That is powerful magic.

Rose's lips purse. "It's an aptitude in my family."

Mace nods. "You're from the bathhouse next door, correct?"

"Yes."

"You know that the Council will not be pleased about this? That if anyone here says anything about this, they could lock you up?" Mace asks.

The women around us gasp in dismay, but Rose nods. She's aware that her abilities can be prosecuted.

Mace gives her a brilliant smile that has my beast wanting to strangle him.

"Well, Gideon, you should get your mate out of here before the Council enforcement show up."

Panic flares.

"She's not my mate."

Mace's eyes widen in alarm and when I turn to face Rose, it's a punch in the gut. Her face has gone pale, and she reels back as if I've struck her.

As if I've hurt her.

Fuck.

"Rose—"

"I-I need to go," she interrupts and flees before I can stumble over any of the words in my mouth. The sound of the bells on the door jangling sears through me. She's gone.

"What the hell, Gideon?" Mace is livid.

If even easygoing Mace can recognize the impact of my statement on Rose, then I've really botched things.

"I didn't want to spook her." It's the only thing I can think to say.

"Not a fish, Gideon!"

"What should I—"

Mace interrupts. "Go fix it!"

I look at the women and the blank face of Jackson. "But—"

"I've got this handled." Exasperation makes Mace's words harsh.

I hesitate. I trust him, but the consequences—

"Go!"

CHAPTER 21

ROSE

Stupid, stupid, stupid.

Pain stabs through my chest with merciless precision and I want to scream, or curl into a ball and sob. If I needed any further indication that I never felt for Jackson what I feel for Gideon, this is it. When Jackson ended things, it had hurt. My feelings or my pride, they had been the same.

But this.

This is heartbreak.

She's not my mate.

Why does it hurt so much? I know this couldn't last forever, but why did I think we had something special? Why had I thought that someone like Gideon wanted me for something more than a sexual arrangement?

Because he said so! He said he wanted something more together. He gave me a courting present!

A sob catches in my chest. I guess that sentiment stopped the moment it came to introducing me to his friend.

I walk through the lobby. The beautiful tile work and décor blurs in front of me. Jared is there with Lowell, looking worried. I throw up a hand when they start to approach me and keep moving.

"I'm going into the main area. Stay out for the rest of the night if you want to see me in the same way after."

My cousin and brother freeze, and I start taking off my clothes as soon as I'm out of their sight. I drop things with no thought of where they fall. The balmy air of the public bathing room touches my bare skin, welcoming me.

A group of regulars are messing around in the pillows. They stop at the sight of me tugging off my leggings.

"Rose!" Wanda sits up from the fray, thrilled.

I sniff.

"Oh honey, are you okay?"

I shake my head; I can't speak without releasing sobs and I'm sick of grieving because the men I engage with don't consider me worthy. The pain twists into anger.

After Jackson, I shut down part of myself. I'm not doing that this time.

I'm going to use pleasure to numb this awful pain and hot anger. I'm a sensual witch. I work in *the* sex hotspot in the paranormal world. There is not a single thing wrong with me.

If any man thinks so, they can go fuck themselves.

"Oh, come here. We'll start with a cuddle and Jason can show you a new trick he learned with his tongue." She reaches her hands out to me and the waggle of her eyebrows has her partner laughing.

The offer should sound salacious, but it's just warm. These are my people. Acceptance is sweet and tears frustratingly prick my eyes.

"Rose!" Gideon's growled shout echoes off the walls and everyone jumps, including me.

I spin on my heel and sure enough, Gideon stands in the entryway. The power of him filling the room the way it always does. Part of me aches at the familiar sensation, a large part, and it makes me even more angry.

"Rose," he says again, quieter. "I need to explain."

"Hey, this is a naked area only," Wanda says. I glare at her.

Gideon immediately starts stripping and I grit my teeth. Goddamn horny women. The rest of the regulars watch the drama unfold in front of them intently as Gideon violently removes his clothing.

"I don't want to talk to you. Actually, I'm canceling our agreement so you can just turn around now." My voice sounds throttled and raw. My anger swings to sorrow and back again in a disorienting way.

"I can't do that, Rose." Gideon tosses his underwear to the side.

"Maybe she should forgive him." The appreciative whisper comes from a woman behind me and it's almost funny but mostly frustrating.

"Yes, you can. It'll be easy. What am I to you except an easy lay?"

I flay myself with the words. Anyone can see the wounds I carry now. The wounds I hid for months just waiting for them to heal. I'm not hiding anymore.

"Don't say that about yourself!" He roars his words and I jolt. Gideon starts walking toward me. All my bravery and strength fades on the choke of a sob. I can't do this right now. My body reacts to the advancing predator, I turn and flee blindly.

I should have remembered that running is a dare to be chased.

I scream as I'm caught, but it isn't arms wrapping around me. Tentacles snatch me off my feet and pull me back. I hit water and warm flesh all at once.

"Get away from me, you overgrown fish!" I snarl and thrash. We're in the main bathing pool. Gideon wraps himself around me and I turn to face his bare chest. We bob in the water.

Gideon coughs. "Now that's just hurtful."

"Fuck you!"

The sob that had been trying to escape breaks through me. I hit his firm chest and start to dissolve.

"I am so sorry, little witch. I said the wrong thing."

I choke as I try to speak. "Y-you didn't lie, we aren't mates."

A sound of anger rumbles through his chest.

"Yet. I want us to be mates."

"I don't believe you!" I shout.

"I didn't want to scare you off, little witch—"

"Don't call me that! I deserve a man who wants to claim me in front of others."

"I'll claim you in front of whoever you want," Gideon snarls.

I don't know how to respond to that. Maybe if the logical part of my mind were present, I could process his words, but I'm just a wounded animal right now. I only want to hold myself tight and wait for the pain to end.

"Okay! Enough gawking, everyone."

I sink down in the water at the sound of Jared's voice but when I peek toward him, he has a hand over his eyes. "Let's give Rose and her man some privacy, alright? Feel free to move to the private rooms to continue your group fun."

A collective groan goes up from our spectators and my cheeks burn.

"But he said he'd be willing to claim her in front of everyone."

"That's so romantic."

"Holy shit, honey, can you spell up some tentacles sometime. I think I've discovered I have a serious thing for them."

"Anything for you, my dove."

Eventually the main room empties along with all of the commentary of the people I know so well.

"Are you okay, Rose?" Jared asks the room and I sniff.

Gideon tightens his hold around my shuddering body. "I had to agree to let your brother castrate me if I upset you, so I'd appreciate it if you give me the opportunity to talk things over with you first."

"Would it grow back?"

Gideon makes a noise in his throat that resonates with discomfort. "It's never been something I wanted to risk, but if you required it—"

"No! I don't want that." Alarm flavors my words. Gideon would do that for me? Impossibly, the offer loosens the tight part of my chest. "It just, this hurts so much."

I press my hand against my chest, against the ache that feels as if my heart has been ripped open.

"Oh Rose, that was never my intention."

"Rose?" Jared calls out again.

All at once, the anger deserts me. My body aches with weariness and pain. I don't want to push Gideon away right now. I'm too weak.

"It-it's okay. Thanks for checking."

Gideon's body relaxes at that. I press my face into the skin of his chest. The tears won't stop, and my energy reserves are fading fast.

Oh.

I groan. "Energy drain."

Gideon kisses my hair and strokes my back. "I figured you were going to come down soon. We can talk over logistics later. Just know I'm sorry, and I don't plan to let you go. You're it for me, Rose. Let me take care of you."

It sounds so good. Like bacon in the morning or the first sip of coffee. So good, so comforting, I'm not prepared to believe it's anything more than a wonderful dream.

We drift in the heated bathing pool as my dreams fade into reality and back again. Floating, twirling, dreams that pull me down until nothing matters but the soft strokes on my back and Gideon's soothing voice.

CHAPTER 22

GIDEON

The energy drain hits Rose hard. One moment she's crying tears that rip at my soul, and the next she's out like a light. I'm just glad I reached her first. I didn't want her to spend a single second longer than she already had, thinking that I don't want her.

Everything after that is a future discussion. Rose is going to be out of it for a while. I take care to dry and dress her and myself before leaving the main bath area to grab her bag from her office. The sight of my courting gift on her desk delights my creature.

Focus, Gideon.

"What do you think you're doing?" Rose's brother, Jared, asks. Stopping me before I enter the public bathing area again.

"I'm going to take care of her. She's experiencing energy drain, so I'm going to take her back to her home and put her to bed."

Jared's mouth tightens. "You guys were in a fight last I saw."

"And she let me apologize before the worst of the drain set in."

"Leave it, Jared. She likes him," Lowell says from his place at the front desk.

After a moment, Jared nods. "Just remember what you promised."

"I never forget my promises." Especially those that remove parts from my person. If I had been thinking clearly at all, I might have hesitated before promising that. Maybe.

I get some looks from the people I pass on the street as I carry a passed-out Rose home. The one she isn't aware I know the location of. Because she doesn't know that I watched her.

There will be many confessions once my mate wakes.

I unlock the door to Rose's place, a brownstone-looking building, before entering. The inside holds the same aesthetic of the woman in my arms. There's no doubt that this is her home. The décor varies from the classy carved wood banister to random scatterings of crystals perching on any flat surface, keeping a large amount of houseplants company.

Streams of sunlight fill the space and the very air is different. It tastes of Rose's brightness and has a soothing effect. It's like breathing a small amount of her magic.

I carry Rose around her home, trying to find her bedroom, and snooping. I take in every fascinating detail and match it to things she's told me about herself and her family.

I find the witch workshop that she and Jared share, Rose said that Jared doesn't practice much so sharing is more convenient. The room looks like a cross between an apothecary, a library, and a craft corner with another collection of her paper products.

There's a cozy sunroom in the back with plants that Lowell comes and cares for to sell as potion ingredients on the side. The stack of books next to a wicker chair indicates that Rose likes to read in this room.

This house is very much Rose's home, and she acts as the base for the Love family.

Finally, I climb the stairs and find her bedroom. Thick candles gather on various surfaces and I peer into her attached bathroom to see even more candles. White candles, pink candles, black candles. Whole spectrums of candles that no doubt have significant meanings. Rose's space isn't messy, per se, but a small amount of clutter adds a lively touch to the room.

I gently set my mate on her bed, which is an echo of the very plush bedding from the bathhouse, before I look around and pick out several candles and crystals marked for recharging.

The action of lighting the candles is so reminiscent of how Rose and I start a session that I have to take a breath to settle the spike of arousal in my body. This isn't the time for that. This is the time to care for Rose.

"Gideon?" Rose's voice is scratchy.

"How do you feel?"

Rose blinks and goes to sit up in the bed before falling back down with a scowl on her face. "Like I've died and was dragged back."

I flinch at the joke.

"I'm surprised you're even awake right now," I say.

Rose makes a gesture with her hands before using them to cover her face. "We Loves are a hardy bunch. The candles also help. I'm still really tired."

"You should sleep. Do you have a type of tea you want?"

She peeks at me through her fingers before sliding her hands down. "You'll get me tea?"

Exasperation is sharp but I soothe myself by twining my fingers through hers. "I'd take on any trial or tribulation for you. Yes, I'll get you tea."

"There's one meant for this, it's in the pink canister." Rose gives a long blink, as if she's on the edge of falling back asleep. I lift her hand to my mouth, giving it a chaste kiss.

"I'll be back."

I put the kettle on and look through the cabinets before finding the dented pink canister of custom mixed tea. There is a helpful index card of brewing instructions nestled in the loose leaf. By the time I find where Rose stores her diffusers the water is boiling. The actions of tea making are wonderfully simple, almost meditative.

I set a timer for the steeping and my phone buzzes. I answer without looking; I know who is calling.

"So, how's your witch?" Mace starts in with no introduction.

"Sleeping off the energy drain. How's the scene?"

"I wasn't asking about that." Mace sounds annoyed and my lip twitches at his nosiness. Mace sighs. "The scene actually went as expected after your drama went down. The officials have taken the women to get their statements. I snuck one woman a burner phone and my card just to be on the safe side, but they seem to be in good hands."

I make a sound of agreement at his actions. Mace continues.

"Jackson is in cuffs, ones that will stay on this time since he has no will of his own for those nifty markings of his to work. I vaguely mentioned a self-destructing artifact that could enact a soul bind and the enforcers just nodded and noted it. No one is going to lose sleep over this guy being bound."

No will of his own, no feelings, no motivations. The binding left the man alive, but most would argue that the life he'll have won't be much of one.

"That's good." I don't think Rose will lose sleep over Jackson, but I make a note to address it. To assure her that her actions were called for. If she needed assurance anyway, the fierce face she wore when she'd enacted the bind comes to mind.

There's a snort over the phone. "I even remembered to pick up the amulet we started this all for."

I blink. I'd forgotten all about the amulet. I'd found a treasure much more valuable on this job. There's a pause in the conversation that Mace breaks.

"Soooo?"

I let Mace sweat it out and carefully remove the diffuser from the mug. The steam wafts up and sticks to my skin.

"Goddammit, Gideon, did she forgive you for being an ass?"

I still and sigh. "No, I don't think so. Not quite yet. We still have things we need to talk over, and my words hurt her."

The truth is a heavy thing. Rose might have cried against me before the energy drain hit but I won't assume that means I'm forgiven.

"Ah, well, best of luck there." Mace sounds tired and I hear the breaking of glass in the background. Mace must cover the receiver because his next words are muffled. "Asa, hitting the alcohol doesn't mean actually hitting it. Go back to your calming breaths or I will restrain you."

I stand straighter. "What's going on?"

Mace huffs. "Oh, now you want to gossip?"

"Is Asa alright?" Concern spikes. Asa is a friend, one that values control over all things. We might not be as close as he and Mace are, but I do care about him.

Mace sighs. "Not really. You aren't the only one dealing with relationship issues. I might have spoken too soon about Asa settling down with someone. I'm just checking on you now because I think this situation is going to get worse before it gets better."

Mace lowers his voice. "I've never seen him like this before."

Apprehension bears down. Asa is no slouch on the power scale.

"If you need a hand, let me know."

Mace's laugh is hollow.

"You, my friend, have enough to worry about. Let me know if you resolve things with your witch and then you can offer your help. I'm monitoring the situation here."

"Still, if you need me—"

"Yes, very well. If he truly loses it, I'll call you."

After that promise, we make our goodbyes and end the call. Now is the time to take care of my mate.

I place a mug of tea on the bedside table.

As anticipated, Rose is already asleep. I order food for both of us from the local deli.

I struggle with indecision for a moment; I don't want to wake Rose, but the tea will help her bounce back. I let the steam waft in front of her face until her eyelashes flutter and I'm looking into her hazel eyes.

She hums sleepily. "You came back."

"You should drink some of the tea."

Rose sighs. "Can you help me sit up?"

I help her up enough that she can sip the tea. I ache to cradle her, but resist the urge. This isn't the first time I've played nurse to another person, but with Rose I'm equal parts wanting to take care of her and tempted man. The strongest temptation isn't even for sex, but to wrap my arms around her as she sleeps.

Rose finishes the tea with a wince before setting it down. Without her asking, I help her lay back down. As if she can read my wants, she grabs my hand before I pull away.

"Lay down with me?"

I freeze. "Are you sure?"

"I need a cuddle. It will help me feel better."

As if I need any more incentive. She rolls into me as soon as I sink into the bedding and emotion rises in my throat.

As always, holding Rose against me feels like perfection, but the sensation is amplified in this place. In her home. It's like all the venturing, greedy pieces of me and my life are falling together with her calm, it's peaceful.

This woman deserves everything.

CHAPTER 23

ROSE

The feeling of completeness is the first thing I notice when I wake. That, combined with the familiar smells of home and the heat of the body under my cheek, spreads comfort through me. I try to connect the dots of how I got here, and my thoughts groggily fall into order.

Jackson's horrendous crimes, the women, Gideon's painful words.

I start to pull away when I remember it all. Gideon tackling me in the main bathing pool. Apologizing. My emotions swing tiredly, and I peek up at the man I've been cuddled up to.

This is the first time that I've ever seen Gideon asleep. He doesn't look less powerful, not really, but there's a relaxation in his face that bleeds into my psyche. This is intimacy. Seeing an ancient creature like this, completely unguarded, is a gift I never expected.

I look away, trying to work through my feelings. My room is illuminated by dawn-colored sunbeams. Orange dim light hits candles that have burned themselves out. Those details, and my need to use the bathroom, tell me that I slept through at least one night.

I ease out of the bed carefully, but Gideon's arm tenses around me.

"I need to go freshen up." Why am I whispering?

Gideon sighs, but releases me before seeming to go back to sleep.

I stare at myself in the mirror after using the toilet and washing up. I look okay for having performed some serious magic. Surprisingly okay. My coloring is good with no dark circles under my eyes. My hair is a little matted, which I contribute to spending a night cuddled up to my kraken—not mine. Gideon.

He isn't mine.

My emotional turmoil is a clashing discomfort that offers me no answers. Gideon apologized for the words that had felt as if they had skewered my heart, but everything is tender now and my bruised soul doesn't believe the things he told me when he was apologizing.

About wanting us to be mates. Something that's probably not possible anyway.

I blink at my face in the mirror. The tea. The reason I don't feel like I've been raised from the dead is because Gideon took care of me. One part of me wants to run away while the other wants to cuddle in bed and never face the world again.

I still have time with Gideon. Time that I shouldn't waste because I'm scared that I lo—

I *like* him, and that's as far as that thought is going to go with the memory of pain so close to the surface.

Gideon's eyes are barely open when I enter my room again.

"How do you feel?"

"Better. A lot better, thank you for the tea."

Gideon lifts an eyebrow. Stiff, I'm so stiff and awkward. How do I handle this? This arrangement is as fragile as the tips of butterfly wings. For me anyway. Gideon just looks at me with an open expression.

Gideon sits up. "We should talk about things."

My resistance is instant. If we talk about what he said and why I reacted the way I did, it will showcase my vulnerabilities. He might tell me he wants to be mates... or other things I'm not ready to believe.

"I don't want to talk right now."

Worry etches on Gideon's face and I finger the hem of my top before pulling it over my head. The worry disappears as his eyes widen.

"I don't want to think." It's true enough. I pull off my leggings then. "You're wearing too many clothes for this."

I strip out of my underwear and Gideon is in motion, removing clothes. Before I can blink, he's an expanse of warm skin. I fall into him. We kiss and I could cry in relief at the stir of arousal in my body. Gideon groans into my mouth, his arms wrap around me tight. It isn't close enough and I push him back on the bed before straddling him.

Lust hits the air as a flavor of something about to sour.

Is this manipulation? Or just me trying to shore up my defenses?

I taste him, sampling and nipping to get what I need. Our bodies move together, skin against skin, and I feel Gideon start to harden under me. My mind begins to coast easily instead of stutter over every detail and punctuation of inner ache.

Gideon squeezes my ass and grinds me against him in a way that lacks the grace that he seduced me with before. His actions are hungry, a little desperate. I break our kissing to wrap a hand around his cock and moan at the hot feel of him.

"Rose," Gideon groans.

"I love how you feel inside me." I tilt my hips to grind against his thigh, wanting to get lost in this. I stroke him and sigh at the same time he does. It's so satisfying to hold him in my grip.

My mouth waters. I've been remiss. This man has given me a plethora of orgasms with his mouth and I've yet to return the favor. The idea of tasting him there, of sucking on his cock until he loses his mind catches like a shiny object.

"I wonder if I'll love your taste too."

I start to slide myself off Gideon's lap. His hands wrap my arms, stopping me.

"Rose—" he says into my hair.

"I want to."

"I hunger to feel you. I was so worried when you stormed in yesterday. I want to feel you from the inside out."

Heat blooms as I remember just how much he's *felt* me before.

His words sound like begging, the only type of begging Gideon can do. I'll make him beg for my mouth later. If there is a later. I hum and let him pull me deeper against his lap, rubbing my wetness over his hardness. The friction has a sigh falling from me until I freeze.

I push back. "Not inside me—" I break off, not knowing what to say but my hand goes to my bare neck and Gideon's brows crease in concern. I left my charm to prevent pregnancy back at the bathhouse.

"You…?" He trails off before flinching. "You're not sure about me."

Anymore. It's there, unspoken.

I lick my lips and blink, trying to vocalize my hang-ups. "Before… was great, but I just—I just can't risk that right now."

My heart resembles roadkill. The idea of having a piece of Gideon forever had been a lovely thought when we'd done this before. Even fully accepting that we wouldn't be together forever, it had been something I was willing to risk.

But now… everything is too raw. Too painful. That lovely possibility is more like a biting snake, striking where I'm unprotected.

Gideon's grip on my hips increases before relaxing. He rocks his forehead against mine, a sad tenderness taking the place of my clumsy overture. The kindled arousal starts to bleed from us.

"We don't have to stop—"

Gideon makes a sound that interrupts me.

"You aren't comfortable with me, Rose."

I can't respond to that statement.

"And we need to talk," he says.

I shake my head, but Gideon continues.

"I have feelings for you, Rose. If we have sex right now, it will mean different things to you than it does to me, and we should be on even footing when it comes to our intimacy."

Irritation loosens my lips. "Just because you can't play breed—"

"It's not that." Gideon's breath is warm against my face and he brings a hand up to cradle my cheek. "Wearing that charm is your right. Asking me not to spill my release inside you, is your right. I welcome you wearing that charm until you decide you want to take it off again, but this relationship of ours is based on more than just sex."

My heart shrinks in on itself, wanting to believe his words, but hesitating, expecting pain.

"If we talk, it's going to hurt."

Gideon's face cracks into a smile. "Oh, so the sex was to distract me. I'm honored."

My cheeks burn in embarrassment, the tears welling in my eyes just make it worse.

"Hey, little witch, breathe." Gideon brings me into a naked hug and I greedily accept the warmth and comfort. "Your feelings aren't the only ones at stake. There are things that I don't want to admit to you. Things you deserve to know."

My curiosity piques. What could he possibly need to admit to me?

"And you could be... experiencing effects from the drain still," Gideon hedges. The reluctance in his voice is almost funny when I make sense of what he's trying to say.

"Are you saying I'm being hysterical, Gideon Strand?" The suggestion that this tidal wave of overwhelming emotion could just be a side effect is a relief. A reason I can point to no matter how close or far from the truth it is.

"Never." Gideon blushes. "But it wouldn't be a terrible idea for me to make you more tea and for both of us to eat some real food."

A warmth settles in my chest and muffles the doubts in my mind.

"Five minutes?"

Gideon presses his face into my hair and breathes in. Obviously, we're both enjoying the cozy skin-to-skin contact.

"Five minutes."

***

I groan in delight as I take another bite of sandwich. A sound has my attention snapping to Gideon. He's frozen in the act of brewing some more tea. His eyes hooded, watching me, a blush stealing over his cheeks.

Embarrassment has my face starting to burn, but a silly happiness pushes it out of the way. Our *activities* this morning may have stalled out, but Gideon still wants me. I try not to smile but I must fail.

Gideon snorts. "Eat your sandwich and stop tempting me, little witch."

The endearment wraps around his words. Yesterday I told him not to call me that, screamed it actually, because every time he does, it's as if it steals a little more of my heart. I swallow my bite of food and take another, trying to not dwell on the state of everything.

The sandwich had been waiting in the fridge for me. Gideon ordered the food last night, though I have no memory of any of that happening. It's another demonstration of how he takes care of me.

Gideon's actions have always been clear.

His words... not as much. I steer my thoughts away from yesterday.

The food helps with my mass of emotions. My heart feels less eviscerated, my soul less battered.

Other concerns occur to me embarrassingly late.

"The women last night?"

"Mace says that Council enforcement took them in and will get them to where they need to be. He made sure that they have a way to contact him just in case."

Gideon places a mug of tea on the table, and I accept it gratefully. It's a tart tea, one of Jared's blends, but it buoys my energy up a level with each sip.

The mention of Mace brings up yesterday. I met Gideon's friend and ran away devastated. My cheeks burn. What a way to make an impression.

"I'm glad that they'll have some support." I almost snort my tea as a very important detail arises in my mind. I cough. "And Jackson?"

"Jackson is now in custody. No one is looking for a soul-binding witch. No worries from that end."

"Good." The response is weak. I'm glad that the soul binding isn't going to come back to haunt me. I don't regret it. I can't.

We're rounding back to other topics now.

Gideon's face goes serious, as if he can sense my nerves. Am I so transparent?

"Rose, I'm so sorry I said you aren't my mate. It was wrong."

I shake my head. "It's not a lie."

Gideon glares before smoothing his face. "Yes, it is. I consider you my mate and I shouldn't have said any different just because I've been waiting to bring it up with you."

His sure statement steals my breath. "What?"

Gideon winces. "I was attempting to not… spook you."

"Spook me?" I ask, but I know exactly what he means. I've kept this man on tender hooks our entire arrangement. Getting close, only to take a step back when emotions come up.

"Rose, I've known I've wanted to keep you since the first moment I saw you."

I blink at that before narrowing my eyes. It sounds too good to be true. Especially with a hanging detail. "When you visited the bathhouse?"

Was it pure chance? No, not according to the way Gideon's eyes cast to the side. The ancient being in front of me doesn't answer right away. Instead, he fidgets, running a finger over the wood grain in the table.

"I saw you before then. I approached you at the bathhouse by design."

I sit back in my chair, confused. But parts of our first interaction are coming back to me.

My nature is greedy... it wants what it wants, and that's you.

Our first meeting had been strange. I hadn't dwelled on it after because the date we'd gone on had felt so natural in comparison. Gideon clears his throat.

"I saw you a week before I approached you. I knew then that I wanted you as my mate."

Surprise freezes me. *A week?* The memory of the sensation of being watched rises in my mind but Gideon isn't done with his confession.

"My nature wanted to be forceful. Claim you quickly. But I also knew if I didn't approach you slowly, I could risk scaring you off... so, I followed you."

"Followed me?" I squeak.

Days of looking over my shoulder. The presence that I felt but didn't fear.

Gideon looks up at the ceiling. "I do believe 'stalked' might be more accurate."

"For a week... your kraken wanted to claim me."

"Not just my inner nature, Rose. At the beginning, yes, it directed me. It cut through any doubts my mind could summon. But it's all of me that wants you to be my mate. For me to be your mate."

Things are starting to fall into place.

"You knew where I lived before bringing me home."

Gideon cringes. "Yes."

The agreement between us. The dates. The courting gift.

"Somehow you knew I wasn't interested in dating. That's why you approached me to match us."

I blink.

"The whole time. You've been seducing me for the long term, the whole time," I say. The stunned words are quiet. "But we can't even be mates."

My mind returns to the subject of immortals and soul bonds.

Gideon rears back. "What do you mean?"

I wave at the air around him. Air that is empty of colorful ephemeral threads.

"You don't have soul threads. We can't bond if you don't have soul threads."

Confusion creases Gideon's brow.

"Soul threads? Wait, you see soul energies?" he asks.

"It's how I make my compatibility assessments. And you don't have any."

Gideon adjusts in his chair, seeming to realize something. The gesture is awkward. "I—uh—cloak."

"What?" I squawk.

Gideon scratches his neck.

"It's a natural reaction for me. It keeps humans and most paranormals from noticing me on a day-to-day basis. To hide my true nature, I cloak everything."

Disbelief thunders in my ears. I never asked. Asking would have meant voicing my wants.

When I open my mouth, I actually laugh. It's an odd laugh, hollow with an upward inflection

"This whole time you've had soul threads?"

Astounding.

"I didn't know you wanted to see them. Or could see them, really."

We fall silent, trapped in the pause of our discussion.

A part of me wants to demand Gideon to reveal himself so that I know, know if we are a good match. But the sensible part of myself realizes that it doesn't matter. I may have gone into this arrangement blind, but that was only one sense. All my other senses know this man.

Since the beginning of our acquaintance, I've been able to experience something with Gideon that I may have missed if I knew our compatibility. I am a matchmaker, but the way I make matches isn't the only way for love to bloom.

Seeing Gideon's soul threads now won't deny how we work together. Not having my usual sight gave me an invaluable opportunity. The opportunity to play, truly spend time with him without being given the answer outright.

It let me be the one to decide, rather than an analysis.

Calm sinks into my bones, finally dispelling the last flailing thing in me that feeds on my insecurity. It could be the food, the tea, or the man in front of me, but I take a cleansing breath and I'm myself again.

"You stalked me." The statement is clear but neutral. In truth… I like it. It helps the fragile belief that Gideon really wants me. "And you want to bond? To be mates?"

The possessive glint in Gideon's eyes gives me a shiver and his knuckles are white. As if he has to clutch his own hands to keep from reaching out to me.

"More than I can eloquently say." Gideon's statement has the hair on the back of my neck rising. It's so intense and perfect that I push down my doubts.

Determination fuels me.

"I have some personal issues—don't interrupt," I say, and Gideon closes his mouth with a snap. "Some things you've helped me with and others… I don't recognize them as being wounds until they're poked. When you denied us being mates it shouldn't have hurt so much. We hadn't spoken about anything official. It was my own insecurities that caused the most pain."

Gideon doesn't say anything, just waits patiently for me to finish though his jaw is so tight I can tell he's tempted to deny it.

"I'm trying to give you full disclosure. There are thoughts in my head that are going to pop up and try and sabotage this." I make a gesture between us. "I don't want to let that happen and I'm going to work on it."

"This?" Gideon asks and I'm almost confused until his pleading tone clicks.

"Us. I want to be with you, Gideon Strand. I'm just saying it won't always be easy."

Gideon breaks into motion, plates clatter. I'm in his arms before I can blink, he sets me on his lap, hugging me to his chest.

"Anything, my Rose, will be more than worth it to be yours."

Yours. Mine.

"But… you don't want to read our compatibility?" he asks.

I snort. "I'm curious, but it doesn't matter. I claim you with what I know and the feelings I have for you."

"Because I'm your perfect match," he says the words with such forceful aggression I can only smile.

My perfect match. The term had been a sore spot, but now it echoes through me with a beautiful resonance.

"You're the match I choose, and that makes it perfect."

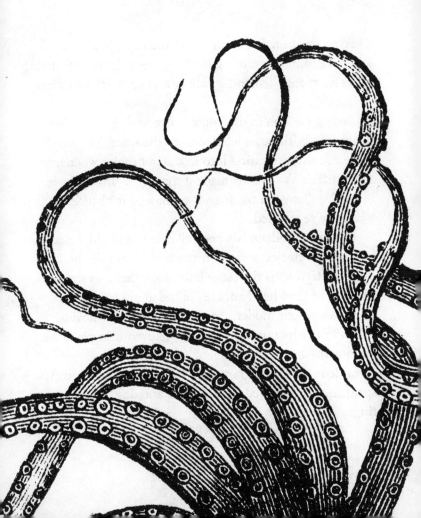

CHAPTER 24

ROSE

After our heartfelt confessions, the day is a lazy one. I still have some lingering side effects from the energy drain, side effects that demand cuddling and naps. It's all rather wonderful.

Seeing Gideon in my home is like finding a missing puzzle piece. There's a wholeness to the space. We watch some television, pausing it to talk about topics whenever they surface. We haven't made it through a single movie, but we've discussed the friends we have, our histories, where we've traveled.

Of course Gideon has been all over the world. I make him tell me stories of the construction of temples in one country versus the cathedrals of another and the varieties of food he's had. He's talked about his favorite things about our modern age, the internet and movies, versus things he misses, the sense of adventuring into the unknown.

Gideon tells me of how he, Mace, and their friend Asa spent the last hundred years finding and destroying slave rings.

"We've slowed down the last decade. It hasn't been as prevalent of an issue and we've made our enemies. Asa took the brunt of the reputation. He's a little more flashy and domineering than Mace and I are," Gideon says, running his hand over the bare skin of my legs on his lap.

I prop myself up with my elbow on the couch cushions. "But you still do it?" I ask.

"When we come across it. It's more of a passive thing now. Are you concerned?"

I look down my nose at him. "I trust you to understand the risks going in. I won't stop you from helping others like Corey when you can."

Gideon's smile is soft and we go on to different topics.

I didn't expect this man to walk into my life and there are still so many facets about each other that we don't know. It won't change my mind about us though.

"I want you to move in," I say. It occurs to me that I should be nervous about asking.

"Okay, is there room for an office or should I rent a separate space?"

I sigh out in relief and smile.

Gideon chuckles. "What, did you think I'd say no? I'm in this for forever, Rose. I won't hold back with you. My inner beast has never felt so settled, so *whole*."

The ease between us expands and pushes back the anxiety that hangs out at the edge of my vision. I won't let that anxiety enter this cuddle.

We have time to figure out the specifics. We haven't even said 'I love you.' It's actions versus words again. We're making plans of spending our lives together before even confessing the words.

I know how I feel.

"It would be polite to apologize for stalking you." Gideon's words hover before dropping like feathers over my skin and distracting me. I move so I can cuddle up to him. The heat of his body sinks into me through his serviceable undershirt.

I hum. "Do you feel sorry?"

Gideon stills and doesn't answer.

My mouth twitches and I pull back to see his face. The mix of emotions are hard to read but he doesn't want to admit that he's not sorry. He spent a whole week watching me without my knowledge and he doesn't want to confess how much he liked it.

Like it was a guilty pleasure.

"I think… that I liked it." My voice is a purr and I press against his body. "There was some sort of sense in the back of my mind that felt like I was being watched. It was annoying, because I kept checking over my shoulder. Kept feeling aware. It's almost as if my body was waiting for you to hunt me down."

Gideon hugs me into him more and his pupils dilate.

"Stop trying to seduce me, Rose. You're resting today."

"But I'm feeling rather invigorated by our cuddling." I tease. "And I'm being honest. The more I remember about all those times the back of my neck itched, the more I'm thinking of your control snapping and you chasing me down."

The idea of being chased, of being claimed, is a tease for myself and shortens my breath. Claimed! Gideon can really claim me, the desire for that pulses through me with urgency. The grogginess from the energy drain had my mind so scattered that I'd forgotten. I don't have to pretend like I can keep him because he'll be mine.

Gideon's muscles are stiff against me. His body on edge. Well, so am I.

I throw a leg over and straddle Gideon. A thrill goes through me at the rub of his wool slacks against my inner thighs and the thin sweat shorts I'd thrown on after this morning's failed seduction.

We discussed our issues. This seduction will not end the same.

The action of straddling my boyfriend—my mate—on the living room couch is so domestic that my feeling of happiness expands.

"Rose," Gideon warns.

I press my body flush against his, cradling his hips against mine. Wanting to grind, wanting friction, but Gideon doesn't move. I brush my lips against his.

"I'd want you to chase me down." I swallow, trying to keep my voice even. "To claim me."

Gideon grips my hips, fingers digging into my ass. His eyes look dark, the way they do sometimes before he loses control. "You're still recovering."

"Please."

I brush my lips to his again and my kraken snaps.

His hand slides into my hair and grips, tugging me in to complete the kiss I'm teasing him with. Gideon sucks my lower lip in with a groan that I echo. Our kiss is hot and wet, the heat builds in me from the barely restrained primal nature I sense under his surface.

Gideon slows the kiss to a drugging pace. It's delicious until I realize what he's doing. What's missing.

I break the kiss.

"You're holding back," I accuse. "You've been holding back on me the whole time. Being careful not to show your hand and scare me away."

Gideon's eyes narrow. "Rose—"

I make a noise in my throat. "Stop trying so hard to seduce me and show me that greedy beast you've been taunting me with."

I gasp as Gideon's hips roll up into the vee of my spread legs. He holds me to his hardness and my eyes roll at the breathless sensation of the contact.

"You want me to stop holding back?" Gideon's voice is impossibly deep and rough over my senses. I whimper at the wave of power that comes off of him. "You want to appease that part of me?"

I dig my nails into Gideon's shoulders through his shirt and start clawing it off of him. He lets me remove it and I run my hands over the skin I uncover; letting my fingers follow the curves and dips of his lean strength.

"There's something my creature remembers, little witch. You broke a promise to me."

I still, confusion clouding my mind at his dark tone.

"You promised that you'd stay away from the auction."

My eyes widen and Gideon snorts.

"You didn't even remember that you gave me your word. My creature is demanding to punish you for the slight. So, little witch, are you so sure you want me to stop holding back?"

I lick my lips. A weight pulls me down at his words, his suggestion.

"What kind of punishment?"

CHAPTER 25

What kind of punishment?

The glazed look in Rose's eyes captivates me. My little witch likes this kind of play and I tuck that detail away. An arsenal of seduction for my lovely mate.

What kind of punishment, indeed.

I hadn't been exaggerating.

My creature's banked anger bites at my control. It did not forget that Rose broke her promise, it had merely been biding its time. The whole day while relaxing with our mate, the darker part of me had been waiting, wanting.

Rose saying she didn't want me holding back had stirred the creature, just like when I'd seen her on that first day. It's awake now.

"It wants a sacrifice."

Rose's brows raise but her face flushes.

"What kind of sacrifice?"

My creature wants a bond. Hell, I want a bond, but I refuse to do that as a punishment.

I smile coherent enough to still tease. "Not the virgin kind."

Rose bites her lip and my creature surges. This morning she taunted me with the idea of her mouth on me, taking me. *That*.

"On your knees." My voice is deep. I'm showing Rose more of that side of me than I have before.

Rose's breath stutters. "That doesn't sound like much of a punishment."

"Think of it as an apology." My creature clamors to the surface at her delay. "So, Rose, are you going to kneel before me and apologize?"

I try to keep a straight face. If this wasn't sexual play, I could imagine how Rose would react with me telling her to kneel. A raised eyebrow and sharp sarcasm maybe. Since this is play, Rose's face flushes and she drags her core down my legs before kneeling on the floor. The action has my cock jerking.

The motion is a mimic of this morning, but I have no intention of stopping her this time.

"And you'll forgive me?" she asks.

A rush of lust has me gritting my teeth to keep my creature at bay. The thought of thrusting a tentacle down Rose's throat until she gags is explicit, but a boundary like that is something to be discussed later. This time, I want her mouth on my cock.

"It'll be a start."

The scent of Rose's arousal hangs in the air. Very much like it had been before our second night together. I almost lost control that night; I straddled the line between wild and feral all for this marvelous witch.

I tug on her hair experimentally and she sighs out a moan. Another detail I catalog.

"What are you waiting for?" I ask.

"You haven't told me what you want me on my knees for." Rose's mouth twitches and I laugh. Her teasing pulls on my dark impulses.

"Your mouth on my cock would put me in a forgiving mood. Don't make me wait."

Rose whimpers and her hands are quick to undo my pants. I inhale at the brush of her fingertips against me. I ache and tense my muscles to keep from thrusting into her grip when she pulls me out.

Her breath teases over the hot skin of my cock before her tongue licks it. The wet slide has a grunt escaping my mouth and my head falls back when she gives another small lick. It's a death of a hundred cuts; each pleasure is a searing sensation.

I raise my head and catch Rose's amused look. Her eyebrow raises in a challenge. I pull lightly on her hair again and she freezes.

"That's a poor apology, little witch."

Her cheeks pinken. "Maybe you should show me how you want it."

This woman might be the death of me, and I wouldn't change a thing. The blood rushes in my ears, my body eager to deliver what she's asking for, but precautions need to be covered.

"Pinch anything you can reach if it gets to be too much."

Rose's pink lips smile, and she pinches the skin of my balls lightly. I jump and hiss.

"Like that?" she asks.

I glare. "Just like that."

I pull her forward by her hair, resting my cock against Rose's lips and she opens to me. The plush lips give way to her hot mouth as I use my grip in her hair to guide her to take more of me. I moan at the stroke of her tongue against me as she sucks.

I push deeper and Rose struggles a little before easing more of me into her mouth. I let her up to breathe and she gasps, her lips erotically wet and red.

"Gideon."

I stop. "Yes?"

"Forgive me?" Rose asks before taking my cock farther into her mouth and hitting the back of her throat.

"Fuck!" I try to hold back, to keep from thrusting up at the blinding sensation. I grit my teeth as Rose slides up my length, licking at the underside greedily.

Rose lets me slip from her mouth. "Well?"

"Don't tease." I tug on her hair and she moans. "You put yourself in danger yesterday, crashing into an operation where you didn't have the details. You could have been facing something more dangerous. You're mine, my treasure, and you will be more careful in the future."

Rose's hips squirm at the tone of my voice. Her hand disappears between her legs to stroke herself.

"And you will keep your *promises* to me." My words come out as a hiss.

Rose moans and, gods, I want too many things at once. Her mouth on me, my mouth on her, my cock sliding inside her tight cunt. One thing at a time. For now.

Rose shivers and makes a small sound that is a familiar precursor to her climax, my creature rears.

I tug her hair to get her attention. "No, you're apologizing to me. This is for me, little witch."

Rose whimpers and winces as she tries to slow down the roar of her pleasure. She engulfs me again with intention. My control stutters and Rose gags when I push her too hard. Shame burns but Rose moans around me. The death of me.

"That's it, take it all," I say.

I push her head down and Rose lets me, her body tight with tension. I'm so close, but so is she. We move together and she takes my cock too far down her throat again. This time her gag ends with Rose crying out around me.

My creature rises with the rush of my climax, wanting to mark Rose with a bond. I hold it back. For now.

"That's it. Now swallow." My words are calm, but my orgasm isn't. It rages as Rose drags it from me with purpose, I come on a low groan. The hand not stroking herself claws into my leg as she swallows my cum down her hot throat.

I release Rose's hair and she gasps for breath; her face flush and lips swollen.

Rose climbs up on my lap, panting but determined. She's pulled off her bottoms and drags her bare cunt along my cock, her hands like claws as she tears off her own shirt.

I catch her arms to slow her, enjoying the comedown from my climax and the view of a naked Rose in my arms. She struggles against my grip.

"Please, Gideon." Rose grinds against my wet cock helplessly as I hold her still. Rose stops struggling for a breath. "Please forgive me?"

My lips twitch and I search myself for any lingering trace of demand, any sign that my creature is holding a grudge. Nothing. The talented little witch took care of that.

"I forgive you."

"Then stop holding back!" Her cry is so fierce it surprises me.

The creature stirs, satisfied but always hungry. "I'm not—"

"Yes, you are. You're still being careful with me, like you don't want to spook me." Rose uses my words against me.

"Rose—"

"You're not going to scare me away, Gideon."

The words are soft, and something brews in me.

"If you run from me, Rose, I'll hunt you down."

The logical side of me, the side that's lived among humans for countless years is aghast at my words. They're true but come from my most inhuman instincts. I don't want Rose to be scared of me even if the concept of smelling her fear wakes the hunter in me.

Rose's breath goes shallow. It isn't fear on her face, yet, but lust.

"Take me."

It's a whisper, but the beast hears it.

CHAPTER 26

ROSE

I'm spread naked over Gideon, my body offered up like a sacrifice. I burn under my skin and have the urge to move against this partially dressed man who calls me his mate, but some instinct freezes me. My Gideon is a dangerous being, and the very air knows it.

Gideon's dark eyes pin me and make it hard to breathe. He's mostly kept this part of himself from me but I recognize it. It's like the night I asked him to breed me but more intense somehow. He hasn't done a thing, but I feel caught, owned.

"Mine," Gideon says.

Gideon intently watches his thumb stroke slow circles on my inner thigh. "Rose—"

He cuts himself off with a shake of his head and his eyes lighten, like he's still fighting this part of himself.

Anger cuts through instinct and the unbearable heaviness of want. I've exposed vulnerabilities to this creature and he still wants to hold back?

"I want it all, Gideon. I'm yours. I deserve everything." The words are sharp. Gideon's eyes snap to mine, his gaze dark and possessive again.

When Gideon moves, it's slow. I still stiffen my body to keep from jumping. His hands run up my naked thighs before one reaches up and strokes over my hair. I want to lean into the pet but hold myself still.

The immobility is a struggle. Gideon's hot cock rests against my wet pussy and the temptation to move is a dangerous thing that my primal brain resists to give into. It knows that the powerful creature between my legs *needs* to be the one to make the first move.

Gideon wraps my hair in his fist and pulls my head to the side, baring my neck. Slowly, he runs his lips over my collarbone, my pulse, until he reaches my ear. The warmth of his bare chest against my body almost distracts me from his words but the wickedness demands to be heard.

"I want to devour you, little witch. Hunt you down and trap you forever. Fuck you and fill you with my seed until your very scent is too mixed with mine for anyone to recognize."

I shiver at the scrape of teeth over the skin of my neck. Gideon inhales, the action suggestive.

"I smell how aroused you are. Every terrible and depraved thing I whisper to you makes you even wetter. You're practically dripping on my pants."

I whimper because he's right about how wet I am.

Gideon's smile is cruel. "It would seem that my little witch likes humiliation. Every time I say anything bordering on degrading your heart rate jumps and I taste you on the air."

My face is on fire. He's right. Something about the callous, dirty things he says drives my need higher and higher until the moment that I'll start to beg. That moment is approaching, tears line my eyes, and my breath shakes my body. The primal energy in the air and my torturous need wrestle each other.

"I wonder what other secret wishes my deviant harbors," he says. My heart rate jumps and I tremble.

"P-Please—" I cry out as Gideon gives my hair a pull and I bite my lip to keep from begging again.

"You do beg very prettily. What do you beg for, little witch? Tell me."

"You." It comes out in a rush, but nothing happens and my body strains. To throw myself away from him or toward him, I can't tell.

"Surely you can do better than that."

The words scald and a sob builds in the back of my throat until the craving in my blood outweighs the shame, my inhibitions.

"Your cock! I want you inside me. I want everyone to know I'm yours. I want them to see it." My voice is high and breathless. *I want them to see it.* I hadn't meant to say that, but now the words are out there, and Gideon is motionless.

Shame clogs my throat from admitting my want for exhibitionism. Will this be the thing I'm rejected for?

My eyes fill with tears and I want to curl in on myself. I said it. I confessed it. And now Gideon will know exactly what kind of woman he asked to be his mate. He'll be disgusted—*shut up, Rose!*

Gideon is an adult. If he has issues with anything I ask of him, we can talk about it. I ignore the pull on my hair and glare at Gideon. Daring him to—what? Say something degrading that won't get me hot and bothered?

Instead of looking disgusted, Gideon looks mildly thoughtful.

"You want people to watch? I've never done that before." His face breaks into a grin. "On purpose anyway."

The heat under my skin replaces the hot anger. "Y-You'd do that?"

Gideon tilts his head like a hawk eyeing a mouse.

"I'll consider it. Right now it's just the two of us and my mate asked for everything. Is that what you still want?"

"Yes."

A deep sound comes from Gideon.

"I want a bond." The words are a statement.

My mouth drops open and I can only blink as happiness spikes through me.

Gideon's eyes lighten, struggling for a moment with his primal nature that wants to claim without questions. "Will you bond with me, Rose?"

"Yes!"

Relief lines his face before fierce determination darkens it.

"Coat me in your wetness, Rose. I want no obstacles when I take you."

Does he mean what I think he means? My breathing stutters when his cock pulses against me. I finally give in to the urge to rub myself against Gideon's hardness. I don't grind down, but softly do exactly what he asks of me and slide my desire over him.

My saliva hasn't quite dried, so the flesh between us saturates quickly and I tease myself by pressing Gideon's cockhead to my entrance before retreating, gliding down and up again. He watches my progress from under hooded eyes.

Lying in wait.

On an upward stroke, Gideon grabs my hip with a snarl and thrusts up into me. I cry out and groan at the stretch.

"Gods," I pray. The first harsh thrust only seats him halfway into my body. I will myself to relax and take him, but my body is both hungry and stretched taut, so the process is slow. Gideon's face holds a fierce sort of humor.

"Perhaps now is the time I let you try and fuck yourself down on me."

I pant at the idea of trying to force my body while Gideon watches. I move and struggle to fit him inside of me, circling my hips and bearing down.

It almost works. I take more of his cock but progress halts and my face burns.

The sounds I make are pitiful, being filled like this feels almost too good to care, but I need to take all of him. The sight of him spearing me is erotic, but the portion of his slick cock I haven't been able to take yet acts as a challenge.

"Gideon, please."

"Please what, Rose?"

"Help me take you."

The grip in my hair tightens and Gideon tilts his hips in small pulses that trick my tense body into accepting him.

"Mine," he growls.

"Yours," I pant and finally sink down his full length with a moan.

Gideon sucks on my neck and the strong pull yanks on the strings of my desire. My body winds even tighter and I greedily rock on Gideon's cock, letting the barrage of sensations flow through me.

"That's it, little witch. Take all of me."

I'm barely coherent when Gideon licks down my neck, over the soft area between my shoulder and throat, and sinks his teeth down, breaking my skin. The pain is sharp, but quick. Instinct has me trying to thrash but my kraken holds me tight to him, filling me to the brink.

My climax flashes through me, and I scream at the breaking of the visceral waves of want and desire. Gideon's movements are harsh, thrusting up into me as he keeps his teeth latched until I feel the tug in my chest.

A pull on the threads of my existence. Every sorrow, joy, and want unwinds in me and reaches out. To my mate. The threads of us are weaving together.

I open my eyes and see the process. "Oh."

My own threads range from soft pink to gold and wind in time to the now visibly vibrant emerald threads of Gideon. They braid together and there's a final pull connecting to my heart when the bond forms.

Gideon releases his teeth from my neck and licks over the wound.

I feel him. I feel the instincts driving him, the satisfaction and affection for me. The aching hunger thrumming through him spills into me, gearing my body up again even though I just climaxed. I sink my nails into his shoulders, wanting to claw him to move faster, do more, completely possess me.

"Gideon—" I choke out.

The world spins until my back connects with the plush living room rug. Gideon's cock slides from me. I fight to keep him, squeezing my legs around his body and fingers scratching over his skin, wanting to still be connected.

I don't stand a chance against my mate.

Gideon flips me to face the floor, pulling my knees up under me and keeping my chest to the ground with a firm hand to my back. The gesture echoes of well-earned dominance.

The position is primal and pleases the animalistic part of myself that wants to be claimed by my mate. I'm so open like this, so unable to hide from anything, all my vulnerabilities spread before me and I don't care. I want to give them all to him.

Give him everything and connect everywhere.

I shout when Gideon thrusts in me. The action is brutal and exactly what his greedy beast desires. Feeling the beastly part of him through the bond is intimidating but it's accompanied with his all-consuming need to care for me, to keep me. It's scary and comforting at the same time.

Gideon groans when he's sunk completely inside me, his hips flush to my ass.

"So perfect, my mate. Gods, I can't imagine never having found you."

"We are bonded now. I feel you," I say. Tears burn my eyes.

There's a surge of intense happiness at my words through the bond and it amplifies the claiming thrust of Gideon into me.

"Going to keep you forever," he whispers. It's a promise that constricts around my heart and the fervor of it builds in me with every stroke of his body in me until I'm crying out in another orgasm.

Gideon reaches under me, rubbing my clit and the climax doesn't end, it goes on and on. Emotional and physical waves surge until pleasure screams through the bond and he's rutting into my body.

At the peak of everything, Gideon pulls himself from me and hot fluid spills onto my back even as his body presses down against mine. I let the weight of him squish me into the rug. My mind floats with one fact trying to pull me down.

"Y-you didn't come inside me," I pant out.

I'm not pouting about the fact that he didn't fill me like the other night. I'd never pout about that.

I might be pouting.

Humor tickles me through the bond and Gideon's laugh is soft and breathless.

"You didn't want me to spill inside you this morning. I don't want you to regret a single thing." Sincerity rings through the words and my soul threads.

"Oh." I'm touched with his care. A fuzzy happiness surrounds me, and the world starts to blur, the energy drain from bonding setting in.

Not yet, I blink to try and stay awake for one last detail.

"I love you, Gideon."

Surprise spikes through the bond. The silly man is surprised. I hum in delight before darkness takes me.

CHAPTER 27

ROSE

The fabric of the sheet rubs against my face and I inhale the scent of it. The scent is familiar and brings to mind mornings of sleeping in and sun-filled naps. Cutting through the comforting smell is the green salty scent of a certain kraken.

I crack an eye open to a déjà vu moment of waking after an energy drain with Gideon's arms wrapped around me. This time his heat is at my back and the ache of this energy drain is a sweet one, like the ache of muscle used for the right reasons, because this time it's from bonding with my mate.

My mate.

I have a mate now. I hide the giddy smile spreading across my face in my pillow. Most witches marry or handfast like humans, but I doubt Gideon's inner beast would have been satisfied with something like that.

I'm mated to an ancient sea monster who makes me tea when I ask and gives lovely back massages. And who, apparently, is not a morning person.

Gideon grumbles into my hair and tightens his arm around me.

I snicker. "I'm getting up."

There's a huff on my neck before he releases his hold on me and turns over in the bed. I blink at the sun coming through my window. Had we slept through a full night?

I don't remember coming to bed and we're both naked. I spot Gideon's slacks on the floor of the bedroom that look as if they've been kicked off last minute. I strain my brain, but only remember the sex in the living room and the texture of the rug under me. Gideon must have carried us both to bed to sleep off the aftereffects from bonding.

And now I desperately needed coffee. The tea had been nice. Restorative. But the craving for coffee hits me so hard that I swear I smell it being brewed. I pull on clothes before heading to the kitchen.

Confusion flares, I do smell coffee being brewed. Has Lowell let himself in again? We'll be needing to have a talk about boundaries now that Gideon is moving in.

I round the corner and let out a startled shriek at the sight of an unfamiliar man blowing on a mug of coffee.

"Rose!" Gideon's voice is a bellow, a clatter of floorboards, and he's behind me. When he spots the intruder, his fierce demeanor turns to exasperation. "Mace."

"Good morning." *Mace* salutes with his mug.

I squint. He actually does look familiar. I'd only seen him for a moment the night of the auction. This is Gideon's friend.

"Gods, Mace, you can't just drop in when you feel like it."

Mace raises his brows but doesn't openly contradict Gideon.

"You must be Rose! Gideon's mate." Mace pauses for a moment, as if daring Gideon to contradict him this time.

"Yes, she is," Gideon says.

I can hear Gideon's scowl and something inside me softens at this exchange.

"Good! So glad you fixed your lapse in judgment."

My lips twitch at the honest relief in Mace's voice and Gideon huffs.

My mate kisses my cheek. "Coffee?"

"Yes, please," I murmur. Gideon walks into the kitchen and I clear my throat.

"Gideon—"

He blearily turns toward me and by some miracle I see past my naked mate to catch Mace hiding a smile.

"You should put on pants." My face is burning at the sight of Gideon's relaxed, bare body.

Gideon creases his brow, as if he honestly hadn't noticed. A moment later, sweatpants appear. The effortless use of magic startles me. Knowing Gideon is more magic than not and seeing it are two different things. It's beginning to hit me that for all that I love him, and that we're bonded, we have a lot to do in the ways of getting to know each other. The concept is invigorating as much as intimidating.

Gideon must see some of the thoughts on my face or maybe he feels it through the bond because his mouth kicks up in a teasing grin as if to say, *just try and get rid of me now, little witch*.

Mace makes a hand motion, inviting me to take a seat at my own kitchen table.

"Oh, I see you've both made it official. Congratulations!"

My attention snaps to the intruder in my kitchen and I see him squint at the soul bond between Gideon and me. Seeing soul threads isn't that common of a trait. I take in Mace's own soul threads and compare them to that trait before my morning brain delivers me the answer of what kind of paranormal being he is. Demon.

"Thank you." I sit and Mace pulls out a chair across from me. The demon does a double take at the crook of my neck.

"Gods, Gideon, you bit her?"

My face heats, but Gideon places a mug of coffee in front of me and I wrap my hands around it like a lifeline.

"Yes." Gideon's voice is matter of fact and I peek at my mate to find him blushing.

"I mean, that's how shifters bond." I hadn't questioned the action.

Mace snorts. "Yes, but that's shifter magic. We could have done the process without it. It would have been... cleaner."

A tinge of shame reaches me from our bond, and a protective urge straightens my spine.

"It happened the way that felt right for us. I have no regrets."

Mace's face lights up, as if my tone hadn't sounded threatening. "Good, good, good."

"Not that I don't appreciate this visit..." Gideon's voice is dry, his patience flaking away. "But what are you doing here, Mace?"

Mace beams at us. "I'm just checking in. I wanted to make sure you didn't need any assistance to make a bond."

Confusion stills me before I make the connection. Demon magics are particularly good at influencing soul threads. The first demons to enter this plane could only stay with the help of soul bonding with witches, if rumors are to be believed. It's no wonder that human mythology remembers them as trading souls in exchange for demon deals.

"But I see that my presence isn't necessary for that. The bond you two have is quite strong, I don't think I would have been able to weave a better one. And the result on both your lifespans would still be a toss-up."

"What do you mean?"

Mace's brows shoot up.

"Did you two not talk about the effect on your lifespans once they were connected?"

Gideon takes a sip of his mug, calm in the face of my panic. "I accepted whatever outcome there would be."

What does that mean?

Mace looks as annoyed as I feel. "You didn't think she should have a say in it all?"

Gideon glares at Mace. "I'm not losing Rose now that I've found her. I have accepted any change to the span of my life."

I wave my hand to dispel the tensions between the two.

"What about our lifespans?"

Mace leans back.

"They're linked. Like most soul bonded beings."

Relief empties my lungs, that means that whatever the outcome, our lifespans will match.

Mace continues, "But things like immortality aren't shared easily. I'd say, best-case scenario, you both may have spans as long as other long-lived individuals." Mace gestures to himself. Demons can live for hundreds of years, but they aren't immortal.

"Worst-case scenario, both of you will live witch-length lives."

Witches generally lived a little longer than humans. A stab of something echoes through me. Frustration? Anger? Sadness?

"You gave up your immortality and didn't think we should talk about it?" I ask.

"Thank you for the visit, Mace." Gideon's eyes are flinty. "I'll call you later."

Mace raises his hands, like this situation wasn't his fault. And it really isn't. He winks at me and pops out of sight.

I blink at the rare teleporting ability before my simmering emotions bring me back to my mate.

"When were you going to bring up the fact that being mated to me will be the death of you?" The phrase sounds more dramatic than it did in my head but it's true.

"You're angry."

The emotions in me crackle and want to snap at this man, except his statement is full of awe and he presses a hand to his chest. I take a breath and Gideon's eyes meet mine.

"I like this, picking up how you feel from our bond. I never thought it would be something I'd have."

I narrow my eyes at him. "You're trying to distract me."

Gideon closes his eyes for a moment and the peace on his face is distracting. Some of his emotions must trickle through to me because all of the sudden my anger deflates and all that's left is aching sadness. Gideon's eyes snap open.

"No, I don't mean to distract you. You've been the best sort of distraction since I met you." Gideon pulls me onto his lap effortlessly. The warmth of him melts me.

"I didn't mean for you to sacrifice—"

"Shhh, it's not a sacrifice," Gideon cuts me off.

I shake my head. "You've given up—"

"But I get you."

"Gods, let me finish!"

Gideon looks suitably sheepish, but now that I know he won't interrupt, I'm at a loss for what to say. The words rise out of me as if summoned.

"I didn't want to cost you anything."

Gideon rubs a hand down my back, waiting until I give him a nod that I'm done. All the diatribes I thought I'd hash out just match that statement.

"Little witch, I've lived lifetimes over and over again. I've seen people close to me grow old and then die too many times to count. I never thought I'd be able to have this."

Gideon gestures to the bond between us.

"A mate. A partner. You are my greatest treasure. As costs go, my immortality is a small price to pay to be able to keep you. To live and die as you do." Gideon pauses before cradling my cheek in his hand. "I love you, Rose. Let me pay this price."

My breath stutters from me, and I blink away tears. I press my face into his neck. The wave of affection from our bond makes it hard to speak and it takes a minute for me to feel the tension in his body, the hope flavoring our connection.

"I love you too."

Gideon sighs out in relief and I give a wet laugh. "I told you yesterday. Why are you so surprised?"

"You whispered it after the high of bonding and sex, excuse me that I wanted to hear it again just to be sure."

I pull away to see his face and a smile teases my lips.

"We do need to get to know each other better."

Gideon's eyes darken and his lust strokes me lightly through the bond. "That can be arranged."

I laugh. "I know you sexually pretty well. I'm talking about as a person. You owe me some more dates, Gideon Strand."

My mate's eyes light.

"We're just getting started, little witch."

EPILOGUE

ROSE

"Rose."

"Just a minute," I say.

"We're going to be late," Gideon responds.

"Keep interrupting me and it will be two minutes."

I finish the email and click send. Satisfaction blooms in my chest and I look up at my mate leaning on the doorjamb of my office. Gideon lifts a brow.

"Are you ready now? I did clear this day and *time* with you." The amusement filtering through the bond ruins the lecturing effect of his words.

"I've done it."

Some of my joy must reach Gideon because his face softens.

"I never doubted you could."

I've cleared my entire backlist. Every hopeful applicant has been matched to the best of my ability. It's taken months, and my email will probably fill up again by tomorrow, but I've finally fulfilled my goal of coupling up, and some surprise throuplings, all the people who've been waiting for a match.

I sigh.

"And now it's time to celebrate," Gideon says with a waggle of his brows. He strides over and pulls me out of the office chair, wrapping his arms around me.

"Oh, so the surprise that you've been planning for weeks is a celebration now?"

I slide my hands up his chest.

"Who says I've been planning it for weeks?"

"I just know."

It's hard to keep secrets when bonded, though I've been told that all bonds behave differently. Some couples can't sense each other's emotions at all and are relieved about it.

I love how much I sense Gideon through our bond.

And my family is shit at keeping secrets.

Gideon narrows his eyes. "Do you know what my plans are? I'll have you know, I used to be very good at hiding things."

I have some guesses, nothing concrete, but I do know that the public room is reserved for a private event and Lowell has been making eyes at me. Annoying 'oh just you wait' eyes.

"I'm not prepared to make any assumptions at this time," I say primly. I have my own surprise for my mate.

"Well then, shall we begin?" Gideon holds up a blindfold and my breath catches.

"Please."

Gideon's dark eyes disappear, and the silk of the blindfold slides against my skin, cool and smooth. Already, the thought of him watching me, seeing me when I can't see him has a tickling heat traveling over my skin.

I know my mate much better now. I know he likes watching me as much as I like being watched. Sometimes the sensation of being watched will come out of nowhere.

It's foreplay while I stand in line to pick up takeout or peruse a bookshop.

Gideon's breath warms my lips before he kisses me. I sigh into the kiss but it's over before I properly taste him. I make an annoyed sound and my mate laughs.

"Patience, my treasure."

Gideon picks me up in a bridal carry and I cling around his neck.

He scoffs. "I won't drop you, I'd just rather you not trip."

I scrunch up my nose as Gideon's steps echo off the tiles of the lobby. "I don't think you'll drop me, you surprised me."

"That *is* the plan."

The air becomes more humid, and I know we've entered the public room. Quiet whispers spark my curiosity.

Gideon carefully sets me down and I hear the rustle of his clothes. It's the familiar sound of him undressing. "Nothing I've planned is outside of what you've said you'd like, but just say the word and we'll stop."

"Not on your life," I say. A woman laughs a space away. I might recognize who if my heart weren't trying to beat out of my chest.

Gideon places my hands on his bare shoulders before he kneels in front of me. I squeeze his muscles in excitement as Gideon carefully removes my sandals first. Then the scrape of his calluses run up my legs, slowly lifting the dress I'm wearing. The fabric drags against my body erotically and I bite my lip to keep my sigh in.

Thumbs slip under my panties and tug them down until they fall to the floor and I step out of them. A hush falls over the room now and Gideon resumes sliding my dress up, exposing me. My face burns and Gideon rises.

We've never done this before.

We've watched others, and shared small touches that could possibly be seen by other bathhouse patrons, but never have we *performed*.

My breath hitches at the new nerves racing through me.

Gideon's hands still. "Okay?"

My nod is quick. I may not know how large our audience is, but I want this. I want to be claimed in front of everyone.

Satisfaction flows through the bond and I'm sure Gideon is smiling at me. His hot hands squeeze my waist before he pulls the dress over my head. My bra disappears with no pause and I'm completely bared to our mystery audience.

My mate's hands run over my breasts, squeezing them in a way that creates an ache low in me. Each pluck of a nipple drawing my core tighter and tighter.

I start at the sensation of something familiar wrapping around my ankles. I gasp at the implication. "Gideon, are you sure?"

Using tentacles during sex is something we both enjoy but Gideon has always said it's something personal for him. I never dreamed that he'd be okay with doing this in front of people.

His affection fills me as a hard pinch has me moaning.

"My mate wants to be claimed in front of others. What kind of kraken would I be not to fuck you the way only I can?"

"But—"

Gideon puts a finger to my lips, silencing me before running it over my cupid's bow.

"It's something I don't want to share with the masses. But these are your people and they've become my people too."

"Oh." I'm touched. The patrons of the bathhouse are our people. Our community. It's a special place with accepting people.

"Do you want me to take off the blindfold now?"

I nod eagerly and the world is revealed with Gideon's deep chuckle. First, I only see Gideon's chest. I peek around him and a group of twenty or so of my favorite regulars are strewn around on bathhouse cushions.

It's quite an audience even if some have gotten distracted with each other already.

"Thank you," I whisper but some people still hear and the crowd snickers.

Gideon freezes. A hand slides to my throat.

My bare throat.

"Rose." Gideon's face is blank, but I experience his awe. His hope.

"Surprise," I sing.

He swallows. "Are you sure?"

After we bonded, I went back to wearing the charm that prevented conception. I wanted some time together first to get to know each other. Knowing that my mate would never leave made me want to take it slower.

"I'm sure," I say.

There's a pang of sadness through the bond. "It might never happen."

"Then we'll figure something out. And have lots of practice."

Hunger and need reach me. It's a mix of his and mine. Gideon pulls me in. The kiss is vicious and a little desperate.

"You're blocking the best view, Gideon!" a male voice teases and I nip Gideon's lip when he stops devouring my mouth.

"You've distracted me." His tone is dark but teasing.

"Then I guess you should get the show on the road."

Gideon moves so that I'm the one now on display. Someone whistles in appreciation when a thick tentacle wraps around my waist and lifts me up. My back rests against Gideon's front and other tentacles spread my legs open.

"Oh gods," I swear.

Gideon directs my hands behind my back and another tentacle restrains them together, giving my back an arch. The audience can see everything. Embarrassment clogs my throat.

"You're already so wet," my mate says.

A tentacle slides up through my folds, not penetrating yet, just providing teasing contact. I shiver.

"Do you think I'll breed you this time? Or should I fill your body over and over again until I do?" Gideon taunts me before that tentacle enters me.

From the crowd, a gasp breaks into a moan and I pant.

"Do you think they want to see how your cunt looks dripping with me?"

"Yes," I whimper.

Gideon grunts and I feel the tentacle pulse and the squish of fluids inside me. The tentacle must be Gideon's hectocotylus, the one that can fill me, continuously, with his seed. We did, in fact, have a discussion about cephalopod anatomy.

Embarrassment heats my face. This amount of release is only the start.

"That's right, you love when I fill you up."

More and more of Gideon's sex organ enters me and the stretch has me starting to squirm. I gasp in surprise when another tentacle slips inside me, spiraling with the first.

Gideon starts stroking my clit softly and my body eases, opens to accept more.

"You love when I fill you up everywhere. Isn't that right, little witch?"

The second tentacle slides from me wetly and teases my ass. Sliding slickness over the puckered opening.

"Oh fuck."

That limb stills.

"Don't stop! Please, Gideon, I want it," I beg.

"That's what I thought." Gideon kisses over my mating mark. The tentacle presses against my ass before pushing in slowly. Anal play with tentacles is the best. All the teasing and stretching with none of the sting of fingers.

The tentacle filling my pussy pulses again as if really trying to fill me to the brim with Gideon's cum. I tense around the wet heat. My cheeks heat as the excess fluid leaks out of me, titillating the spectators.

"Jesus Christ, I hope they do this again."

"Tentacles are my new favorite thing."

A moan builds in my throat. Gideon's hands come up to my breasts, plumping them up for the crowd as if he can read my mind along with reading my emotions.

"My mate likes having an audience."

I cry out as the small end of a tentacle replaces Gideon's fingers on my clit; swirling and sucking at it like a wet mouth. My desire is pushed higher and higher. I thrash in neediness but the tentacles restraining me hold tight.

I'm so full. Claimed. Loved.

"Yes, my treasure. You are mine. My beautiful, wondrous mate."

Gideon groans and pulses again inside me. He could do this all night, continually mate with me, filling me over and over again, but I don't have that kind of stamina.

"Please, Gideon—" I scream when the tentacle in my pussy forces in more and *twists* just right. I break, my orgasm a wild endless thing, pushed longer and longer until I'm gasping.

Gideon sucks on my mate mark tenderly. I rest my head back, my mind floating on a cloud after my release.

"Another."

"What? Gideon—" I break off on a moan as suckers move over my clit and Gideon continues to throb and stretch my limp body. The touches are soft at first, but he builds the tension in me up again just as easily as a master with an instrument.

If I broke before, I shatter into pieces now. My body mindlessly moves, sounds and sights are too much to comprehend.

I fall back on Gideon, completely limp.

Gideon pulls from my pussy slowly and a rush of fluid has a helpless moan escaping my lips. The tentacle teasing my ass leaves too. My body burns in embarrassed satisfaction. Replete in love and deviancy.

The air rushes in my ears and suddenly hot water surrounds us. The sound of the splash echoes in the room but I'm in too much of a daze to notice anything until Gideon has massaged the muscles in both my arms. I'm tucked against his chest now, the wet skin warm against my cheek.

"Gods, Gideon, are you trying to kill me?" I rasp.

"Never. You're the one that decided you wanted to play breed-the-willing-witch."

I snort and take a peek out at our audience. "I don't think they miss us."

The crowd has broken out in an orgy.

I'll take that as a compliment.

"How was that?" Gideon asks, as if he can't feel my love and fulfillment through the bond. His lips curl in a satisfied smile.

"Give me a moment. I'm seeing stars."

"I wanted to do something special for you."

My heart is so soft it's practically goo.

"Nothing has ever been more perfect."

THE END

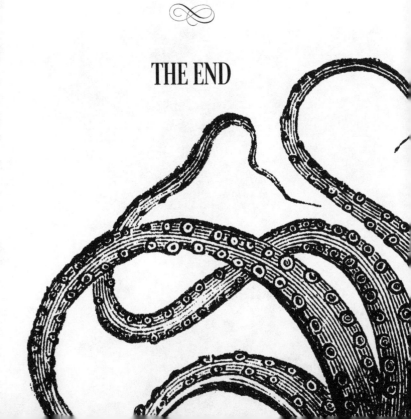

Note from the Author

Hello Dear Reader!

Thank you for taking a chance and reading Stalked by the Kraken!

I have a confession. This book was written on accident. I had a list of next books to write and thought that the story of how Sophia was banned from some bathhouse (a detail mentioned in Three of Hearts) would make a fun, short side story to the series... It did not end up being a short side story.

During the writing of this book, I waffled on whether I should actually publish it. I've read and loved plenty of sci-fi tentacle books but no paranormal tentacle romance books. I seriously wondered that maybe this would be too weird.

So, I'd now like to thank the readers on TikTok for helping give me the confidence that people do want more monster romance in their life. The tentacle scene in A Lady of Rooksgrave Manor by Kathryn Moon also went a long way in reassuring me that this would be something that some readers would adore. Thank you, Kathryn Moon, for writing that!

A thank you to Liz Alden and Kate Prior for beta reading this book and pointing out the things that needed more depth and time. You guys helped make Rose and Gideon into a favorite love story of mine.

As always, thank you, Dear Reader, for reading my book. It's always a marvelous thing that people read the books that I create and I'm grateful to you.

L. Lark

About the Author

Lillian Lark was born and raised in the saltiest of cities in Utah. Lillian is an avid reader, cat mom to three demons, and loves writing sexy stories that twist you up inside.

LillianLark.com

Printed in the USA
CPSIA information can be obtained
at www.ICGtesting.com
LVHW091749261123
764962LV00046B/568